ELEMENTALS 5

THE HANDS OF TIME

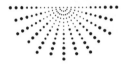

MICHELLE MADOW

CHAPTER ONE

I stepped into the swirling time portal and screamed. My soul felt like it was being torn from my body. It was like someone had reached inside of me, grabbed onto my soul, and was peeling it out of every inch of my skin. I was floating through nothingness, unable to see anything around me, unable to feel anything but the excruciating pain.

I'd traveled through many portals before—ones that had taken me to the cave in Kinsley, to Greece, to Antarctica, to LA, and even to the prison dimension of Kerberos.

None of them had felt like they were tearing me to shreds. Was this portal killing me? Chronos had told us that traveling through the time portal would take away one year of our natural lives. Did I not have one year left? Was this pain happening because I was dying? Was this what death felt like?

Then, as quickly as the pain began, it stopped. Solid ground formed under my feet, and I found myself back in Kerberos, standing next to Danielle, staring at the backs of Ethan and Blake's heads as they waited next to the portal that had taken them to the prison world. Ethan's grip was tight around Blake's body, his knife pressed to his neck.

But despite the danger, all I cared about was that Blake was here. *Alive.* Happiness flooded through me at the sight of him, making all the pain from the time portal disappear at once.

A shadow glided ahead and floated off to the side— Erebus. As promised, he'd shifted into shadow form immediately after coming through the time portal, and was off to distract the dragons.

Then Ethan's knife vanished from his hand.

"Hey!" He flexed his hand and stared at it, as if that might make it appear again. "What happened to my knife?"

Taking advantage of the moment of surprise, Blake elbowed Ethan in the stomach, head-butted him in the chin, and escaped his grasp. He spun around, slamming his fist into Ethan's face over and over again. They were so involved in fighting that they didn't even see Danielle and me standing to the side.

I raised my bow, an arrow already strung through and ready to shoot. But I had no more magic arrows left, and the guys were so close to each other as they fought that I couldn't risk aiming for Ethan and accidentally shooting Blake instead. So I stood ready, waiting for my perfect opportunity to strike.

Ethan spun around and aimed a punch at Blake, but he must have been dizzy from the blows to the head, because he missed. Blake ripped the bag with Medusa's head in it off Ethan's back, tossed it to the side, and got another punch in to his cheek. Danielle hurried to the bag and grabbed it. I followed behind her, my arrow still poised and ready to shoot.

Ethan spat blood to the ground and looked up, finally catching sight of Danielle and me.

"Nicole?" He rubbed his head and glanced at the portal that led back to Earth. "Danielle? But you didn't come through the portal. I would have seen it...I was watching. How did you get here...?"

Blake dropped his fists the moment Ethan said my name, turning to look at me. He looked just as confused to see me as Ethan. I didn't blame him—after all, Danielle and I had just literally appeared out of thin air.

Danielle twirled a knife in her hand—the knife she'd taken from Ethan's cottage before we stepped through the time portal. As Chronos had explained to us, nothing could exist in two places at once. Anything taken through time would replace the version of it that existed in the past—which was why Ethan's knife had vanished from his hand after we'd stepped through the portal with the same knife from the future.

"Looking for this?" Danielle asked, giving the knife a dramatic swish.

"My knife." Ethan ran for her, but then he stopped. Apparently he realized that despite his strength, he would be at a huge disadvantage in a fight against the three of us without a weapon.

Blake took the opportunity to jump on him from behind, landing a few more punches and capturing Ethan in a hold. But Ethan—a demigod son of Zeus— was stronger than Blake, and it didn't take him long to fight his way free. He ran out of the hold, turning around and breathing heavily to get his bearings. He looked at Blake, and then Danielle, and then at me, defeat crossing his eyes.

"You beat me." He held his hands up, glancing at the top of the mountain. "Put your weapons down, and we'll talk this out. There has to be a compromise we can agree on." He wiped sweat off his forehead and glanced at the cloudy, amber sky again, squinting his eyes as if he were searching for something.

"Looking for Helios's solar dragons?" Danielle asked him.

Ethan whipped his head back to look at her, his

eyebrows scrunched in confusion. "How do you know that...?" he asked, taking a step toward her and looking around. "Where exactly did you come from?"

"*How* I know that doesn't matter," she answered. "What matters is that we have it on good authority that those dragons won't be coming."

"You're wrong," Ethan said, although his voice wavered, his confidence waning.

Blake joined Danielle and me and removed his knife from his boot. "We should bring Ethan back to Kinsley and lock him in the holding room where we kept the siren," he said. "Then we can get to the bottom of all of this and figure out what he knows."

"No." I shook my head, not looking away from Ethan. An image passed through my mind—Blake, in a puddle of his own blood, dead at Ethan's hands. "He's too much of a risk to have around. There's only one way to make sure he doesn't interfere in our mission or hurt any of us ever again."

I pulled back on the string of my bow and shot the arrow straight through Ethan's heart.

CHAPTER TWO

Ethan's eyes glazed over, and he fell to the ground, dead.

I slung my bow around my back and turned to Blake, wrapping him in a hug and crushing my lips against his.

"Blake," I said his name, so happy that he was here, alive. I kissed him again, needing to remind myself that this was real. He kissed me back, but more hesitant, as if he were confused about my sudden enthusiasm.

I supposed I couldn't blame him. It had been only minutes since he'd seen me last. It had been *days* since I'd seen him. And only recently, I didn't think I would ever be able to see him again. The image of him dead would never stop haunting my mind, but he was here. He was alive.

Everything that had happened the first time we were in Kerberos was one long nightmare. And with Ethan dead, it would never become our reality.

After knowing what he did to Blake—or what he *would* do to Blake—I didn't even feel bad about killing Ethan.

I was just happy that Blake was here and Ethan was gone.

I pulled back to look into Blake's eyes, needing to reassure myself that this was actually happening. "I love you, Blake," I said, unable to stop the words from pouring out of my mouth. "I love you so much."

I'd waited too long to say it because I was afraid he might not say it back. If my original timeline had stayed the way it was, I *never* would have gotten the chance to tell him how I felt. Which was why I'd done it now.

I didn't know what would happen in the future. But I knew one thing—I didn't want to have any regrets.

He smiled at me, his familiar brown eyes looking down at me as he traced his finger across my cheek. "I love you, too," he said, and I pulled him closer, relief rushing through my veins at the confirmation that he returned my feelings. "I was waiting for the right time to tell you, but you beat me to it."

"I couldn't wait any longer," I told him. "What if that moment in the cave was the last time we ever saw each other? I couldn't live with that. And now that we're finally with each other again... I didn't want to waste any time. We never know what moment might be our last."

"What's gotten into you?" he asked, smiling. "You're acting like you haven't seen me in a month."

"Not quite a month," I said. "More like a week. But it was the most awful week you could ever imagine..." Memories of my time in Kerberos passed through my mind so quickly that I didn't know where to begin. How could anyone understand what a nightmare it had been without experiencing it for themselves?

"Now's not the time to get into that," Danielle broke into our conversation. "We need to get out of Kerberos. Plus, Chris and Apollo are back on Earth right now with our past selves. Wait until we're there to explain what happened, so you don't have to tell the story more times than necessary."

"Okay," I said, since as always, Danielle had a solid point.

"Your 'past selves?'" Blake repeated, his eyes wide as he looked back and forth between Danielle and me. "And you've met Apollo?"

"It's a long story." I reached for his hand and squeezed it. He squeezed back, although he still looked confused. "But yes, Apollo's on the other side of the portal right now, gifting us with items that will help us on our journey through Kerberos. I'll explain everything soon. For now, let's get back to Earth, okay?"

"I'm getting the feeling that whatever happened to the two of you is crazier than anything I could imagine," he said.

"Your feeling's right." Danielle marched to the portal, but she turned around, looking wistfully up at the mountain.

I knew she wasn't going to miss it here in Kerberos, so there was only one person she could be thinking about—Erebus.

"He'll be fine," I told her. "Remember how easily he pulverized that dragon?"

"I wasn't worried about him," Danielle said. "Of course he'll be fine. He's a primordial deity. I just..." She took a deep breath and tossed her hair over her shoulder, refocusing on me. "It doesn't matter. Are we going back through that portal or what?"

"This story is sounding crazier by the second," Blake muttered.

"You have no idea," I agreed.

We walked to Danielle's side, Blake's hand not leaving mine. I reached for Danielle's hand with my free one, and together, the three of us stepped through the portal.

CHAPTER THREE

U nlike the first time I'd stepped through the portal to Kerberos, this time I was prepared for the loss of my senses—for the feeling of floating through nothingness. The first time I'd traveled through this portal, I'd panicked. But compared to the portal that had taken me back in time, it was an absolute breeze.

I landed on the ground of the cave, Blake and Danielle's hands still in mine. Apollo stood ahead of us, his back toward us as he presented the Golden Sword to Danielle. The past versions of Chris and myself stood next to her.

But then the past versions of Danielle and me were gone. Vanished into thin air, as if they'd never existed at all. The only thing that remained was the Golden Sword of Athena, which clattered to the ground.

"Whoa." Chris stared at the three of us, then at the empty spots next to him, and then back at us. "How...? When...?" He continued to stare at us, his eyes wide, clearly at a loss for words. "Does anyone want to tell me what's going on here?"

Apollo turned around, his lips curving into a small smile. "Welcome back, Blake," he said. "And Nicole and Danielle... I see you've received help from Chronos."

"Yes." I nodded and glanced at the bag by Apollo's feet. Since I held the Golden Bow in my hand, the version that he'd brought to give to me would be gone. But I hadn't brought the crystal arrows back with me. Were they still in that bag?

"Chronos rarely changes the past himself, let alone allows others to travel through a time portal on their own." Apollo pressed his lips together, studying us. "I can only imagine that whatever happened to you in Kerberos was very grave."

"You have no idea." Danielle walked to the Golden Sword and picked it up, holding it in the air and smiling. "I'm glad to have this back, though." She sheathed the sword, and then she held her palms up to the ceiling, rain showering all around her. She lifted her face to the rain, her expression one of pure bliss. "I'm glad to be able to do that again too," she said once the rain shower stopped.

I gathered white energy, healing all the bug bites, stings, scratches, and every other injury that I'd gotten during my time in Kerberos. "I can use my power again, too." I reached for Blake to heal him—he'd gotten pretty banged up in his fight with Ethan—and walked over to do the same for Danielle. It felt amazing to access the white energy again—as if a part of myself had been restored.

"What's going on here?" Chris asked. "You were both standing next to me, and then suddenly you were gone and coming through the portal with Blake. You're all dirty and look like you've been through hell. Where did you go? And why am I the only one left here?"

"They received help from Chronos—the primordial deity of time itself," Apollo explained. "How far in the future are you from?"

"Not long," I told him. "We were only in Kerberos for a week."

"Except for me," Blake added. "I was there for minutes, at the most."

"True," I said. "It was Danielle and I who were there for a few days. Then we came back, saved Blake and Medusa's head, and came back through the portal."

"What happened during the week you were in Kerberos?" Apollo asked.

"A *lot*." I shuddered at the memories, not wanting to think about them any more than necessary. "Maybe we should explain starting from this moment, when you gave us the gifts the first time around?"

"Yes." Apollo nodded. "Please do."

"I'll summarize as fast as I can, since we only have a week before Typhon rises, and we need to figure out how to stop him," I said. "After you gave us our gifts, we —me, Danielle, and Chris—entered the portal to Kerberos. When we got there, Blake and Ethan were being flown up the mountain by Helios's solar dragons. We tried to climb directly up the mountain to get to them, but it was too dangerous, so we had to find another way."

"There were tons of wildlife on the mountain trying to kill us," Danielle added. "Including the Nemean lion. Even with our weapons, we wouldn't have made it up the mountain alive."

"Did we even *try* to fight them?" Chris asked. "I can't imagine that we would give up without trying."

"Yes," I told him. "We killed a bunch of huge foxes. But you got bit on the shoulder in the process. We didn't know it at the time, but the venom was poisonous. And since we didn't have access to our elemental powers while we were in Kerberos, I couldn't heal you."

"So... I died?" His eyes widened, his expression serious. "That's why I didn't come back through the time portal with you?"

"Not exactly," I said. "The venom would have taken weeks to make its way through your system. It *is* why you're not here, but I want to tell this story in order, so I'll get back to that part later."

"Okay." Chris nodded. "Go ahead."

"After seeing the lions, we turned back to find another way up the mountain," I said. "That was when Erebus found us."

"Of course Erebus gets his kicks out of wandering the hell dimension." Apollo rolled his eyes. "Hopefully he didn't give you much trouble. Since you're still alive, I'm guessing he didn't."

"He was there to help us." Danielle raised her chin, matching Apollo's gaze. "We wouldn't have made it out of Kerberos alive without Erebus there as our guide. We owe him our lives."

"Sorry." Apollo held his hands out in apology, although his voice dripped with sarcasm. "I didn't realize the two of you were so close."

Danielle glared at him and said nothing.

"Anyway," I said, wanting to break the tension between them. "Erebus led us along another, more meandering path that led us to a safer way up the mountain. We faced a lot of trials along the journey—every realm in Kerberos was designed to torture us or kill us—but eventually we made it to the Lair of the Dragons. Since the mountain becomes too steep to climb past that point, we made a deal with the dragons to fly us up the mountain."

"Dragons are notoriously difficult to bargain with," Apollo said. "What did you offer them to get them to agree?"

"The Golden Sword of Athena." Danielle ran her fingers along the handle of the sword, and I knew she was glad to have it back.

"Ah." Apollo nodded. "An offer they couldn't refuse."

"By that point, the Golden Lyre was out of tune, and I only had one crystal arrow left," I explained. "The Golden Sword was all we had that they wanted. So they took it, and they flew us up the mountain. There was a frozen lake at the peak, with the Titans trapped inside. They couldn't do anything to harm us—I don't think they were even aware that we were there—but the ice was starting to crack. Once it cracks, they'll be able to break free."

"You need to close the portal before that happens," Apollo said, his eyes more intense than I'd seen them yet.

"Yes," I agreed. "We know."

"Where was I through all of this?" Blake asked. "You said that those dragons had flown Ethan and me up that same mountain, right? Were we still there when you got there?"

I met his eyes and opened my mouth to tell him, but I couldn't. How did you tell someone that they'd been murdered? Even though it had happened in another timeline, I didn't think I could speak the words without breaking down from the memory of finding his bloodied corpse in the center of that cottage. Just remembering it now was enough to make me re-live the grief all over again.

He watched me closely, resolve crossing over his features. "I didn't make it," he said, his voice strangely calm for such a strong revelation. "Did I?"

"You couldn't access your powers in Kerberos, and it was you against Ethan and the two dragons," I told him. "Ethan didn't even *need* to bring you with him—all he wanted was Medusa's head. He only took you so he could kill you and cause me the same grief that he'd had to go through when Rachael died."

"That twisted monster," Blake growled, his fists clenched to his sides. "Now I understand why you didn't let him live back in Kerberos. If you hadn't killed him already, I would do it myself."

"I had no choice," I agreed. "I had to kill him."

But even though I said it, there was still a part of me that questioned what I'd done. Because I *did* have a choice.

And I'd chosen to kill him.

The scary thing was—I didn't regret it.

"So Blake was dead and Chris was poisoned," Apollo said, bringing us back to the story. "It still doesn't seem like enough incentive to get Chronos to send you through a time portal."

Even though he was my father, I wanted to tell him that he was a jerk for saying that so insensitively. Sure, Blake and Chris were fine now, but he had no idea how torn apart we'd been when we thought otherwise.

But I held my tongue, because he was right. Both of those things *weren't* what convinced Chronos to send us through the portal.

"Ethan also destroyed Medusa's head," I explained. "He gouged out her eyes, making them useless."

"And without Medusa's head, the group of you had no chance against Typhon," Apollo concluded.

"Exactly," Danielle said. "So even though I figured it was a long shot, I asked Erebus if he could contact Chronos for us. He did, and after realizing that the world would end if the timeline remained as it was, Chronos came to us and created a time portal so we could go back and change the past."

"Why did you go back to a point where you could save Blake, but not Kate?" Chris clenched his fists, looking at Danielle and me like we were monsters. "Did you forget about her completely?"

"Of course not!" I said, hating that he thought that for even a second. "The first thing I asked was if we could go back to before the fight with Medusa so we could save Kate. But Chronos wouldn't allow it. He refused to send us back that far because he wouldn't risk the outcome of the fight changing, and us not getting Medusa's head. *He* decided on the point when we returned. We didn't have a say."

"Okay," Chris said, although he still looked uneasy. "So why didn't I come back with you? Was that bite I'd gotten from the fox so bad that I would have been a detriment when you returned to fight Ethan?"

"Mortals aren't meant to travel through time," Danielle explained. "Doing so causes a huge stress to our bodies—it takes away one year of our natural lives. Nicole couldn't heal you since she couldn't access her powers, and because of the bite, you only had weeks left to live. If you'd gone through the time portal, you wouldn't have survived."

"It's probably good that you don't have to remember anything," I added. "What we went through in Kerberos... the things we saw while there... I wish I could go back to before it all and never have to experience it, too."

"I don't," Danielle said. "Everything we go through in our lives—even the hard parts—helps make us who we are. I wouldn't forget anything, even if I could."

I suspected that she just didn't want to forget *Erebus*, but the situation was too intense to joke about, so I said nothing.

"I guess I understand why I couldn't come back with you," Chris said. "But what happened to the version of me that traveled with you through Kerberos? He was just… left behind?"

"As Chronos explained it, the version of you from that timeline ceased to exist the moment we traveled back here and changed the past," I said. "That timeline is gone. You—*this* version of you—is the only one that's real."

"This is heavy." Chris sighed and ran his hand through his hair.

"It is," Apollo agreed. "It's best not to overthink time travel too much, or it will make your head spin. What matters is that your mission to Kerberos was successful and that you're home safely. I was just preparing to give you your gifts, but since you don't need them anymore, they won't be necessary."

"But you're not taking back the sword." Danielle's hand flew protectively to its handle. "Right?"

"No." Apollo chuckled. "The Golden Sword was yours to begin with, so I wouldn't dream of taking it back. And Nicole, you can keep the Golden Bow that you brought back with you, too."

"And the crystal arrows?" I asked, motioning toward the bag. "They're in there, right?"

"They are." He nodded. "And I'm glad to know that they were helpful to you while you were in Kerberos. But crystal arrows aren't exactly easy to come by. And now that you're back, you don't need them anymore. So I'll be holding onto them until they're needed in the future."

"It's too bad we won't be getting our gifts." Chris pouted. "I love getting presents. I was looking forward to seeing what mine would be."

"Nicole or Danielle can tell you later," Apollo said. "For now, there are more important issues to discuss."

"Like what?" I asked.

"I have information that's supposed to be secret to you," he said. "You're supposed to figure it out on your own. But I believe that you deserve a reward for succeeding in your mission through Kerberos, and this information will help you defeat Typhon... so now, I will tell you what you need to know."

CHAPTER FOUR

I didn't know why Apollo would hide something important from us to begin with—after all, it was in his benefit if we defeated Typhon and sealed the portal. But I worried that if I said that, he would change his mind about sharing this information, so I kept my mouth shut and waited for him to continue.

"The Earth Elemental—Kate—was turned to stone by Medusa," Apollo said—as if we could forget. "Immediately afterward, you contacted me through the sun pendant, asking if I could reverse the curse. The next day, you consulted the Book of Shadows, asking it the same question."

"The Book of Shadows said that Medusa's curse is impossible to reverse," Chris said, standing straighter. "Are you saying that it lied?"

"Wait for me to finish." Apollo held a hand out, his gaze stern. "The Book of Shadows didn't lie. It's true that it's impossible to reverse Medusa's curse. However, do not lose hope for your friend. She can never become what she once was, but she *can* become something better."

"What do you mean?" Danielle asked. "Isn't Kate in the Underworld right now?"

"Any living creature turned to stone by Medusa is not sent to the Underworld," Apollo explained. "To go to the Underworld, the soul must leave the body. But when someone is turned to stone, their soul becomes trapped inside the rock, unable to escape."

I gasped, recalling the statues at the art museum in LA that we saw when we'd gone to seek out Medusa. I remembered observing them, wondering if there was still a part of them alive in there, looking out through their stone eyes, aware of the world around them. I swallowed down a lump in my throat at the realization of how right I'd been.

"So Kate's not dead," I said. "She's still in there. Trapped in her own body. Is she aware of what's going on around her?"

"Your friend *is* dead," Apollo said. "Her body will never be habitable again. And as far as I know, she is not aware of her surroundings. Her soul is simply trapped inside the stone, unable to escape."

I shivered, because that sounded even worse than I'd imagined.

"So what are you saying?" Blake asked. "We need to find her a new body? And somehow transfer her soul into it?"

"Not quite," he answered. "However, I recommend that a solid start would be researching the process of apotheosis. Because if the process completes successfully, your friend *will* have a new form."

I wasn't sure what kind of form he meant, but I knew one thing—anything would be better than Kate being stuck in a stone prison of her own body for the rest of eternity. That fate sounded worse than being trapped in the underworld of Kerberos itself.

"And if the process doesn't complete successfully?" Danielle asked.

Apollo's eyes darkened. "Then you will not see her again in this life."

"We'll complete it successfully." Chris clenched his fists in determination. "This is Kate's only chance. We *have* to do it right."

"Whether or not it completes successfully is up to the gods," Apollo said. "But I don't think we should hang around here any longer. After all, time is of the essence, and you still need to figure out how to save the world." He reached down to pick up the bag with our gifts in it, preparing to leave.

"Wait," I said, remembering one last thing I wanted to ask him. "Typhon and the portal aren't our only problems. Back in Greece, we angered Helios when we accidentally killed one of his immortal cows. He's wanted to get back at us ever since—that's why he found Ethan and convinced him to turn on us. He promised Ethan that if Ethan brought Medusa's head to Kerberos and destroyed it, he would bring Ethan's sister Rachael back from the Underworld. Now that Ethan's not around to do Helios's dirty work anymore, what's to stop Helios from coming after us himself?"

"And if he does come after us, how are we supposed to fight him?" Danielle added.

Apollo showed no emotion—I supposed that with thousands of years of practice, he'd learned to control his expressions. But I remained focused on him, praying that he would step up to defend us. After all, he was my father. We might not know each other well, and his parenting methods might be different than those of a human parent, but he *had* to care about me a little. Right?

I held my breath, anxiously waiting for his response.

"If Helios comes after you, you'll have no chance against him on your own," he finally said. "And Helios is a wrathful god. Well—I suppose we all have our moments—but his are particularly bad. He's hated me since I took over as god of the sun. If he comes after you and stops you from defeating Typhon, the consequences would be severe for everyone—including myself and my fellow Olympians. I cannot allow that to happen. Therefore, I will tell the other gods of Olympus about this problem, and together we will take care of Helios. All that you need to focus on is defeating Typhon and closing the portal. Understood?"

"Yes." I nodded, even though Apollo's reasoning sounded selfish and far from fatherly. "Understood."

"Great," Apollo said, swinging the bag of presents that he never gave us over his back. "Congrats again for your success in Kerberos, and good luck on the mission ahead. I don't think you need reminding that the entire world is counting on you."

A light as bright as the sun surrounded him, filling the cave with its light, so blinding that I had to look away.

Once it dimmed out, he was gone.

CHAPTER FIVE

We drove back to Darius's house, where Darius, Hypatia, and Jason waited in the living room. They were all focused on the television. I'd never even *noticed* a television in Darius's house before—but this one was so huge that it would have been impossible to miss. On closer look, I noticed a slit in the ceiling above the television—it must be able to slide out of the ceiling at the touch of a button.

On the television was a breaking news report about an unusual amount of activity around Mount Etna. The reporter on screen said that scientists were calling for an evacuation of the entire province surrounding the volcano in expectation of a major eruption. They predicted that the volcano would erupt around March 20—the spring equinox. Townspeople were shown gathering belongings from their homes, squeezing as much as they could into their small cars in preparation to head out of town.

The news report ended, and Darius turned off the television. It did, in fact, recede up into the ceiling.

"Since you're back in good time, I take it that you were able to use Medusa's head to turn the Cyclops to stone?" he asked us.

Hypatia glanced at the door, her forehead creasing with worry. "Where's Ethan?" she asked, looking at the door again as if she expected him to stroll in at any moment.

So much time had passed for me since we'd left with Ethan to find the Cyclops. It was so strange that to them, we'd only left recently. They had no idea that so much had happened to us since that moment.

"Ethan's not coming back," I told them, bitterness creeping into my tone from just having to speak his name.

"Why not?" Hypatia sat forward in alarm. "What happened to him?"

"Why don't we all sit down?" I said. "Because we have a *lot* to catch you up on..."

CHAPTER SIX

We told them the entire story, and Darius ordered us pizza, realizing that a lot more time had passed for us than he'd initially thought. The hot food was heavenly after living off protein bars in Kerberos for days on end. Finally we reached the end of the story, finishing on our final conversation with Apollo.

"Do any of you know what apotheosis means?" I asked the Elders. "Apollo said that's how we would be able to save Kate, but he didn't give us any more information."

"I do know what it means." Darius stared at a piece of pizza on his plate, making no move to pick it up again. Instead, he pressed the pads of his fingers together, appearing to be deep in thought. Then, after a few moments passed, he looked back up at us, his eyes sharp and focused. "I've never seen it done in my lifetime," he continued. "But apotheosis is the process of turning someone into a god."

"No way," Danielle said. "That's really possible?"

"It's possible," Hypatia confirmed. "Although it's very, very rare. I can only think of a few times in all of history when it's been done successfully."

"But we can do it for Kate," I said, sitting forward in excitement. "That must be what Apollo meant when he said that we couldn't return her to the form she'd been in before she was turned to stone. Because before being turned to stone, Kate was mortal. After we finish this process, she'll be a *goddess*."

"Once she's a goddess, will she want anything to do with us measly mortals anymore?" Chris asked. He sounded like he was joking, but his eyes creased with worry.

"Let's take a step back for a second," Jason said, and we all quieted, looking at him to continue. "I understand that you're excited about the possibility of seeing Kate again, but our primary concern this week is stopping Typhon from rising from Mount Etna. Perhaps it's best to put the apotheosis on the backburner until Typhon has been destroyed."

"No." Chris sat straight, his voice serious. "We're more likely to succeed in destroying Typhon if Kate is working with us. We can't put this off. We need her to help us defeat Typhon."

"It makes sense," Blake pointed out. "Kate's elemental power is Earth. Since we'll need to be at an active volcano to turn Typhon to stone, her abilities could be crucial to our success."

"Good point," Danielle agreed. "Lava is molten rock. Kate's the only one of us who could control it."

"And if Apollo told us that we'll be better off with Kate helping us, we need to listen to him," I added. "He's on our side—not to mention that one of his godly specialties is *prophecy*. He wouldn't have told us that if he wasn't trying to help us."

"Exactly," Chris said, eager to back me up.

"So… how do we start the apotheosis process?" I asked, looking at the Elders for answers.

"That's one of the problems," Hypatia said. "Apotheosis is a dangerous, mysterious process. It's only been done successfully a few times, and each time it was done differently. It's certainly *never* been done to a soul that's trapped inside stone after being cursed by Medusa. We would need time to research before we tried anything."

"So create a portal to the New Alexandrian library," Danielle said. "With all of us working together, there's no reason why we shouldn't be able to figure this out."

Hypatia took a deep breath and gripped the edge of

her seat. I anxiously watched all three of the Elders, hoping they would agree. We needed them to create this portal for us. Regular methods of travel would take too much time, and with only one week until Typhon would rise, every minute was of the essence.

"Twenty-four hours," Darius finally said. "That's how long we will set aside to research a safe way to proceed with Kate's apotheosis. If we cannot figure something out within that time frame, we'll have to move on to figuring out a plan to defeat Typhon."

"Thank you." I let out the breath I'd been holding and twisted my hands together. I was grateful that we had this chance to save Kate. But I was also worried, because twenty-four hours seemed like such a short amount of time to accomplish something so huge.

"We've got this." Blake reached for one of my hands to stop my fidgeting and gave it a small squeeze. "There are seven of us working together. *And* we can call on energy to keep us awake and focused. If we all look in different places, there's no reason why we shouldn't be able to figure something out in that amount of time."

"You're right," I said, grateful for his support. "Let's do this."

With no time to waste, Hypatia created the portal, and we all stepped through to the New Alexandrian library.

CHAPTER SEVEN

The New Alexandrian library was breathtakingly beautiful. Everything inside—the floors, the ceilings, the columns—was made of gold. Even the *rugs* were threaded with gold. The sun shined down from a circular dome in the center, its rays warming up the building. The sight of them made me feel like Apollo was with us, supporting us in this quest for knowledge.

I gazed up, taking in the splendor of the library. I'd never been in a room with ceilings so high. There must have been five floors worth of books, at the least. The first level was full of scrolls, and as the levels increased, the books became more and more modern, until the top where they looked like books I might pick up at the store today. I'd never been much of a bookworm—I preferred being active and outdoors—but even I was left breathless by all the books in front of me.

If Kate were here, she would have been in heaven.

And if we did our job right today, soon Kate *would* be here, able to see this building and get lost in the seemingly endless books for days.

A librarian was working at the front desk—a witch, I assumed—and she nodded at Hypatia when she stepped through the portal. The librarian didn't ask any questions—apparently it wasn't her job to question the Head Elders. But I was glad to find that besides her, and now us, the library was empty.

"Where do we start?" I asked, taking in the endless shelves of books.

"There's a computer room in the back," Hypatia said, leading the way. "It was added in the early nineties—of course it's been updated to keep up with the times—but we keep the room hidden, because computers are such an eyesore in a place as beautiful as this."

"Are all the books eBooks now?" Danielle asked. "So we can read them on the computers?"

"Heavens, no." Hypatia laughed. "The most recent books are eBooks, yes. But only the ones that are also available to the public. Everything else is kept in its original format—although we do, of course, have copies in a secret library that's located in a place only known to a few people. The computers contain a catalogue of all the books in the library. You can search the catalogue, and it will tell you where to find the relevant books in the library. There are also laptops that you can bring with you when you research to take notes."

"Okay." I took a deep breath and entered the computer room, feeling suddenly overwhelmed by the massive amount of material we had to search through. "I guess that searching for 'apotheosis' would be a good start, right?" I asked, trying to focus on one thing at a time.

"Yes, it would be," Darius said. "I suggest that we all search here together and each come up with a list of books that we think will be relevant. After an hour, we'll take a look at our lists and see which books we agreed on. Then we'll find the books and divide them up evenly. While glancing through them, be sure to only focus on the sections that are relevant to our search, since that will speed up the process. But first, I'd like to lead a meditation session. We already discussed that yellow energy will help you focus and retain the material that you've read. But more than just retention is necessary right now. We're looking to generate ideas."

"Which means we'll need violet energy," Danielle jumped in, as if we were in a classroom and she was trying to show off her knowledge.

"Yes." Darius nodded. "And as we know, time is of the essence. So let's do the meditation, and then begin our research."

CHAPTER EIGHT

Hours passed as we researched, and eventually the late night librarian clocked out, replaced by an older lady who I guessed was in charge of the early morning shift. Before we knew it, the sun was rising, casting its pale rays across the golden floor.

We'd been here for more than twelve hours. Which meant we only had a few hours left to figure out a solution.

I was feeling more and more hopeless by the second.

For the past few hours, Blake and I had been sprawled under the dome, a handful of books and scrolls in front of us. Danielle, Chris, and Darius were seated at the tables in the main room, and Hypatia and Jason were in a study room on one of the upper balconies.

We'd been drinking water infused with orange energy to keep us awake, but after nearly twenty-four hours of not sleeping, the exhaustion was taking a toll on my body. My eyes tingled with the effort to keep them open, and I rubbed them to stop myself from nodding off. I yawned and blinked a few times, forcing myself to continue browsing the pages of the book in front of me. I leaned against the wall, the book perched on my legs, and while I would probably feel more awake if I sat up, my head felt so heavy that even moving positions felt like a challenge.

I skimmed through the pages, looking for any mentions of ambrosia. All the stories about people who had gone through the apotheosis process were different, but a few hours ago, we'd agreed that ambrosia—the divine drink of the gods—was our best chance at successfully recreating the process for Kate. The problem was that we had no clue where we could find ambrosia. I was hoping to uncover a map that would lead us straight to it, but so far, I'd discovered nothing of the sort.

The more I searched, the more impossible this quest felt. And sitting inside and researching was making me feel more drained than ever. It didn't feel like we were making any progress. I was focusing as best as I could because this was our greatest chance of helping Kate, but I just wanted to get outside and *do something* to help us move forward.

I'd started to nod off again, but then Danielle screamed for us to come see something, jolting me awake. I slapped the book on my lap closed, not bothering to mark my place, and stood up. Blake was already up, his hands raised above his head as he stretched.

"This better be good," he said, finishing stretching. "I don't think I can stare at these books for much longer."

"Me either." I reached for his hand, needing reassurance again that he was here and alive, and together, we walked over to where Danielle sat hunched over a laptop in the middle of the library. She'd used a pen to bundle her hair into a bun at the top of her head, and she bounced her legs, her eyes bright and alert.

I hurried over to her, optimistic that she'd discovered something useful.

"What did you find?" Hypatia asked Danielle once we'd all gathered around her.

"Something that's going to blow your mind." Danielle lowered the screen of her laptop, clearly not wanting us to see it yet. "Remember how in one of the three main stories of apotheosis that we found earlier, we learned that Dionysus brought Ariadne to the mountain Drios to turn her into a goddess?"

"Yeah," I said. "But didn't we decide not to focus on that story, since Ariadne wasn't given ambrosia?"

"We did," Danielle said. "But I wasn't finding anything about where to find ambrosia, so I figured that it might not hurt to backtrack and look more into the other stories of apotheosis to see if I could find a hint there. I still wasn't finding much, so I decided to broaden my search to the internet. I looked up the mountain Drios, since that seemed to be a key element in Ariadne's transition. I couldn't find anything about a *mountain* called Drios, but when I looked up Drios on its own, I found out that it's a village in Greece on an island called Paros, which is right across from an island called Antiparos. I started researching the different mountains there, which was when I found this."

She flipped up the screen of her laptop, showing us a photo that I recognized instantly.

"It looks just like the caves where the portal to Kerberos is." I leaned down to get a better look at the image. It wasn't of the room where the portal was, but the shapes of the stalagmites and stalactites were nearly identical to the ones in the cave. "But it can't be the *same* cave," I said, resting my elbows on the table as I studied the image. "Can it?"

"This is the photo of the Cave of Antiparos," Danielle said. "According to my research, *this* is the closest cave to the town of Drios, and the entrance to the cave is on a mountain."

"So you think that's the same mountain where Dionysus took Ariadne?"

"Yes." She nodded. "And I think we can safely come to the conclusion that once he took her up the mountain, he led her into the cave. We don't know where in the world the cave with the portal to Kerberos is, since the only way we can enter it is through a portal, but it looks so similar to this one. And both caves have connections to the gods. It's too much of a coincidence —they have to be the same cave."

"They do look similar," Chris agreed.

"So you think we can find ambrosia in *our* cave?" I asked. "That the answer's been right there all along?"

"There's only one way to find out," Blake said, and I stood back up, having a good feeling about what he was going to say next. "We have to go there and search for ourselves."

CHAPTER NINE

J ason created a portal for us to go to the playground in Kinsley next to the cave, and he, Hypatia, and Darius stayed back in the library to continue doing further research. We would call them once we were ready to return and then we could update them about what we found.

The first things I noticed upon stepping out of the portal were the huge footprints leading out of the cave. I gasped, putting two and two together and realizing how they'd gotten there.

"The giants," I said, pointing at the prints in the dirt. "We saw them escape Kerberos when we were there. We knew they were coming. And we were so involved with trying to figure out how to save Kate that we didn't realize we could stop them."

"The witch on guard should have called us the moment he spotted the giants." Chris glanced around the area, searching for the guard. He was nowhere to be found.

I shivered, dreading what that could mean for him.

"It looks like the giants were heading east," Danielle said, looking out at the path of the footprints. "To the ocean."

I let out a breath, since the ocean was the opposite direction of where all four of us lived. And we'd checked in on our families before leaving the library. They were safe inside their homes. They also knew about the dangers, and knew to *stay* inside until we returned home and told them it was safe to leave.

"How long has it been since the giants came through the portal?" Blake asked.

"Hours." I looked at Danielle for verification, since we weren't exactly paying attention to the time when we were in Kerberos. She nodded in agreement.

"We have no idea how far they could have gotten," Chris said. "And we don't have time to track them down right now. We have to stay focused on figuring out how to save Kate. Until then, let's hope the giants keep laying low."

As much as I hated it, he was right. We had limited time, and had to remain focused on the big picture.

Right now, that meant stopping Typhon, and saving Kate.

CHAPTER TEN

W e stepped through the portal that led to the cave, bracing ourselves for anything. After all, who knew what other monsters escaped after the giants? Erebus had told us that more monsters in Kerberos were learning that the portal was weakened, so more of them were trying to make their way through. We had to be prepared for anything.

I expected to see the stone statue of the Cyclops in the center of the cave—since it had been there the last time we were there. What I *hadn't* been expecting was the girl around our age sitting calmly on the ground next to the Cyclops, facing the portal. Her back was toward us, but I recognized that long, wavy blonde hair anywhere.

Rachael.

Ethan's twin sister had died in Greece, in the hydra's cave. The hydra had pierced her shoulder with its fang, the poison entering her system and killing her. Ethan blamed me for not being able to heal her in time, and he'd never forgiven me. Then, when Helios came to him and offered to raise his sister from the dead if Ethan brought Medusa's head to Kerberos and destroyed it, Ethan agreed to the deal.

I hadn't expected Helios to honor his side of the bargain. But now, Rachael was here.

And Ethan was on the other side of the portal to Kerberos, dead.

Did she know about her brother's fate? Was that why she was here, staring at the portal? To mourn him?

"Rachael?" I spoke her name softly, not wanting to make any sudden movements. I had no idea what to expect from her. When we fought with her in Greece, she was spunky and impulsive. But this Rachael wasn't the same Rachael we'd fought with. She'd been to the Underworld and back. Who knew how that could have changed her?

She stood up and turned around, and I gasped at what I saw. Her veins were gray and bloated, spider webbing across her chalky, bruised skin. A hole the size of the hydra's fang remained in her shoulder, coagulated black blood surrounding the edges of the wound.

Helios might have followed through on his promise

to bring her back from the Underworld, but he hadn't healed her body. He'd left her as a walking corpse.

"Hey." Rachael smiled, as if everything were normal. "Are you waiting for Ethan, too?"

"No," Blake said simply. "We're not."

"Oh." Rachael's forehead creased, and she frowned. "What are you here for, then? And where's Kate?" She sounded so normal—*vulnerable* even. If I closed my eyes, I would have had no idea that I was speaking with someone who looked like a monster.

"Kate's not here." Chris stepped up, his fists curled at his sides. "Your brother killed her." He raised his hands and shot a gust of air toward Rachael, lifting her up and pinning her to the cave wall.

She kicked and screamed for him to let her down, but he didn't let her budge. She gasped for air, choking, her face turning more and more purple by the second.

"What are you doing?" I asked Chris.

His eyes were narrowed, glaring at Rachael with no hint of pity or remorse. He didn't respond—instead he threw her back at the wall again, banging her head against the rocks.

"Let her go," I begged. "You're killing her."

"Of course I'm killing her." He tightened his hold on her, and she squeaked as she tried to suck in breaths of air, her eyes about to pop out of their sockets. "Look at her—she's a monster! She shouldn't be here. She should be dead, just like her brother."

Two streams of fire shot toward Chris's palms, and he screamed, dropping to the ground to put out the flames. Rachael fell to the ground, released from his hold. She wrapped her hands around her throat and gasped for air, each breath sounding less and less strained.

The fire was out around Chris's hands now, but his skin was mangled and charred. He stared at them, breathing heavily from the pain, and turned his gaze up to Blake. "What the hell, man?" he said. "You burned my hands!"

"I had to." Blake's eyes were cool as he looked down at Chris. "It was the only thing I could do to stop you from killing her."

Chris raised his arms as if to use his power, but nothing happened. "My hands," he moaned, bringing them back to his lap and staring down at them in shock. "I can't feel my hands. I can't use my power."

"I'll heal you," I told him. "But you have to promise that you won't try killing Rachael again."

He glared at me, saying nothing.

"You're angry about what Ethan did to Kate and want to take it out on Rachael—I get that," I said, hoping to get through to him. "But she's a victim in all of this. She didn't do anything to harm us. We have to hear her out and talk to her."

"Fine," he said through gritted teeth. "Just heal my hands. Please."

I knelt down next to him and placed my hands on his burned ones, calling on the white energy and healing him in seconds. Once I pulled away, his hands were good as new. He flexed his fingers, as if making sure they still worked, and sent a gust of wind through the room. My hair whipped across my face, and the stone statue of the Cyclops blew to the ground, breaking into pieces. Then the air stilled, and Chris stood, his gaze fixed on where Rachael stood on the other side of the cave. She backed up to the wall, her eyes wide in fear. But as promised, he made no more moves to harm her.

Her eyes darted around the cave, and she sprinted toward the tunnel—toward the lake of boiling water. As a demigod daughter of Zeus, she was faster than all of us. But Danielle raised her hands in the air, and water zoomed from the end of the tunnel, freezing into a wall of ice.

Rachael skidded to a stop, seconds away from colliding with it. Then she saw her reflection in the ice and screamed.

"What happened to me?" She pressed her hands

against the ice, as if she were hoping the image in front of her was a lie. "Why do I look like..." She paused, tracing her fingers against the reflected lines of her face. "Like a *monster*?"

I took a few tentative steps toward her, not knowing where to start. "A lot's happened since you last saw us," I said. "What do you remember last?"

"I was in the hydra's cave." She turned away from her reflection and stepped away from it, as if she couldn't bear looking at what she'd become. I couldn't blame her—I would feel the same way. "The hydra pierced me with its fang," she continued, her voice shaky. "Ethan rushed to my side to try stopping the bleeding, but my blood felt like it was *boiling*. The next thing I knew, I was floating above my body. I watched as you tried to heal me, but I knew it wouldn't work. Then a god appeared in front of me—Hermes—and he brought me to the ferryman who took me on a boat to the Underworld."

"What happened after that?" Danielle probed.

"Everything after that is hazy." Rachael gazed up at the ceiling and ran a hand through her hair, as if she were trying to remember. "The next thing I remember clearly is being dropped off here by Helios. He told me to wait by the portal for Ethan to return. I asked him why Ethan was in Kerberos, but he just said that Ethan would fill me in on everything once he got back, and then he was gone. Since then, I've just been sitting here, waiting."

"For how long?" I looked around the dim, cold cave, feeling terrible that Rachael had been here alone.

"I don't know." She shrugged. "Hours, I guess. But what Chris said—about Ethan being dead—it's not true. I know he's in Kerberos, and that it's tough to survive there, but my brother is strong. He'll make it out alive. I know he will."

She looked at the portal with so much hope, and my heart dropped, knowing that Ethan wasn't coming back. And even though we had to kill him to stop him from killing us, he was her brother. How were we supposed to break this news to her?

I glanced around at the others, and they looked as torn as I did.

"Why are you looking at each other like that?" Rachael's face creased with worry, and despite her monstrous appearance, she was just a scared girl who needed answers. "What's going on?"

"Rachael," I said her name again and shuffled my feet, stalling for what was coming next. "Like I said, a lot's happened since we saw you last. I think it's best that we start from after the incident in the hydra's cave."

"You mean after I died?" she asked, surprising me by

how easily she said the words. "It's okay. I know I died back in the hydra's cave. You don't have to pretend that I didn't."

"Yes." I nodded. "We'll start from after you died."

From there, we filled her in on everything.

CHAPTER ELEVEN

R achael stared at the portal to Kerberos, saying nothing. I couldn't blame her. What we'd told her was a lot to soak in. And even though we'd explained that we had no choice—we *had* to kill Ethan to stop him from killing us—I wouldn't blame her if she never forgave us for what we did.

Finally, she turned back to us, her eyes filled with tears. "Just answer one question," she said, her voice quivering as she spoke. "Why did you kill Ethan in *there?*" She pointed to the portal, making it clear that by "there," she meant Kerberos. "Why couldn't you have brought him back to Earth first? At least that way, he would have been sent to the Underworld. Now he's in the underworld of Kerberos, going through who knows what kind of torture, and he'll never see anyone he loved again."

Her question broke my heart. Because she was right. Ethan had done terrible things, but did he truly deserve to be sent to the underworld of Kerberos? Now that I was thinking about it, I didn't think so. If he'd been sent to the Underworld of Earth, he would have been sent to one of the realms there and paid for what he'd done.

But when I'd exited the time portal and seen Ethan and Blake, there had only been one thought going through my mind—I had to kill Ethan before he killed one of us. So that was exactly what I did. In the original timeline, Ethan hadn't hesitated to kill Blake in Kerberos. It hadn't struck me to hesitate in doing the same right back to him.

But that still didn't make it right.

"You're right," I admitted to Rachael. "We should have brought Ethan back to Earth first. I'm sorry that we didn't."

"So get Chronos here," Rachael demanded. "Get him to create another time portal, so you can go back and fix this. I can come with you and talk to Ethan. I'll get him to see everything clearly. I'll bring him back to our side, and you won't have to kill him. I promise you won't."

"It doesn't work like that." Danielle spoke calmly, trying her best to soothe Rachael. "What Chronos did for us… it was a once in a lifetime opportunity. And we set the path right again. He won't risk having the past go any other way."

Rachael's eyes filled with tears, and she looked away from us again. I didn't know what to say to her. What could possibly make all of this better? I glanced over at Blake, but he seemed as unsure as I was.

"We need to remember why we came here," Chris finally spoke up. "We have to find the ambrosia so we can bring back Kate, and every minute we spend talking is another minute closer to Typhon's return."

"I'll help," Rachael said, which took me by surprise. She must have noticed my shock, because she added, "I don't think I'll ever forgive you for killing my brother in Kerberos. But what he did to you these past few weeks… I don't agree with it. I know he wasn't thinking clearly, because he was grieving my death, but what he did was wrong. He shouldn't have blamed you for what happened to me. And if it weren't for him slipping that gray energy into your drinks, Kate would probably still be here right now. The least I can do is help you bring her back."

"Thank you," I said, humbled by her offer. Going to the Underworld must have changed Rachael—she was *definitely* different than the girl who had impulsively run to the hydra and gotten herself killed. Or maybe I simply hadn't had enough time to get to know her before she'd died.

Either way, I wanted to do something to show her my appreciation.

"I can try to heal you," I offered, hoping it would be a start toward earning her forgiveness. "It won't take long. Afterward, we can search for the ambrosia."

"That would mean a lot." She ran a finger across her cheek and grimaced, apparently reminded about how monstrous she looked. "Thank you."

I walked toward her, and she met me in the middle of the cave. The others gathered around, watching. Up close, Rachael looked even worse. I could see every detail of her swollen, discolored veins, just as I had when I'd tried to heal her in the hydra's cave and failed. Even the whites of her *eyes* looked puffy and purple.

I couldn't imagine the amount of pain she'd been in when she'd died.

"What should I do?" She held her hands out, waiting for instructions.

Normally I put my hands on the part of the person that had been injured. Rachael's whole body was affected, but I guessed it would make sense to start with the source of the injury—the place where the hydra's fang had entered her body.

"You don't have to do anything," I told her. "I'm going to put my hands on your injury and call on the white energy to heal you. I've gotten pretty fast at this, so it shouldn't take more than a few seconds."

"Okay," she said. "Let's do this."

I reached for her shoulder, hesitant to touch the wound. Usually when someone was injured, the blood was bright, fresh, and flowing out. Hers was dark, coagulated, and still.

The blood was dead. So was her skin. Gray and sickly, like she was a walking corpse. Which, I supposed, she was.

I pushed away my hesitation and reached for the wound, closing my eyes and laying my hands on top of it. Her body felt room temperature—as if I were touching an inanimate object. No warmth emitted from it at all. I had to open my eyes to verify that I was touching Rachael and that I hadn't accidentally reached for the cave wall instead.

"Well?" she asked. "Did you start?"

"Not yet," I told her. "I'm about to."

I closed my eyes, reaching out with my mind to gather the white energy around me. As always, the energy came to me immediately, filling my body with its familiar warmth.

I tried to send it toward Rachael, but it was like hitting a wall. The energy couldn't sense her. It was like she didn't exist at all.

This had only happened to me three other times—

when I'd tried to heal Blake after Ethan had killed him, when I'd tried to heal Kate after she'd been turned to stone, and the first time I'd tried to heal Rachael when she'd died in the hydra's cave. There only one common denominator. All those three times, I'd been attempting to heal someone who was already dead.

Trying to heal Rachael right now was no different.

I pulled my hands off of her and opened my eyes, unsurprised to find that her appearance was unchanged.

"Did it work?" she asked. "Do I look normal again?"

I shook my head, my heart sinking as her hopeful expression disappeared. "I tried," I told her. "But I can only heal people who are alive. My best guess is that Helios kept his word on bringing your soul back from the Underworld, but he didn't reanimate your body."

"What do you mean?" Rachael stepped back, her mouth open in horror. "He put me back into a *corpse*?" Her hands flew to her arms, to her stomach, and to her face, understanding dawning in her eyes. "I'm cold," she realized. "My body... it's not alive."

"It's not," I agreed, watching her sadly. "I'm so sorry. I did everything I could. I tried to heal you... but I can't bring back the dead."

CHAPTER TWELVE

"What does that mean?" she asked. "I'm going to be a walking corpse forever?"

"I believe the correct term is 'zombie,'" Chris chimed in.

Rachael sat down and buried her face in her hands, as if she were too ashamed to look at any of us. "What am I supposed to do?" She raised her head again, her eyes filled with tears. "I'm hideous. I'm a *monster*. I'll have to live in hiding forever. My life is ruined." She pulled her legs up to her chest and lowered her head in her knees, crying.

I looked at the others, not knowing what to do. I'd already tried to help her—there was nothing I could do to fix her.

"I have an idea," Danielle announced.

Rachael's head shot up, and she wiped away her tears, waiting for Danielle to continue.

"As you know, we came to the cave to search for ambrosia so that we can turn Kate into a goddess," she said, pacing back and forth. "According to Apollo, the apotheosis process rids the soul of its previous body and provides a new, immortal body. Once we find the ambrosia, I don't see what harm it would do to have Rachael test it out first. If it works for her, then we'll know it will work for Kate."

"That should work," Blake said. "*If* there's enough ambrosia for both of them."

"And if there's not?" Rachael asked.

"We'll deal with that if it comes to it," I said, since the answer I was sure we were all thinking—that Kate would get the ambrosia no matter what—was *not* what Rachael would want to hear.

"Okay." Rachael stood up, a newfound life in her step. "Where do we find the ambrosia?"

I looked to Danielle, since this had been part of the plan we'd created back in the New Alexandrian Library.

"Ambrosia is liquid," Danielle explained to Rachael. "And it's consumable, which makes me think there must be water in it. My power allows me to sense all water nearby. I should be able to sense the ambrosia, and will be able to lead us to it."

With that, she kneeled down and placed her hands palms-down on the ground. She closed her eyes and scrunched her forehead, clearly deep in concentration.

No one spoke—I worried that even a whisper would distract her from her task.

A few seconds passed in silence. Then the ground started to shake, and I heard something crack in the nearby basin—the one I'd fallen into when we fought the harpy last winter.

I turned to look at it, and saw that a geyser had erupted in the center, yellow liquid spurting out and up from its vent.

"Well, guys." Chris rubbed his hands together, staring excitedly at the basin as it filled up with the liquid. "It looks like we found the ambrosia."

CHAPTER THIRTEEN

The geyser eventually finished exploding, and now we stared down at the basin full of ambrosia. The liquid shined and shimmered, as if it were molten gold itself.

Rachael stepped forward, smiling down at the basin. "This is it then," she said. "I'll drink the ambrosia, and turn into a goddess."

"It might not be that easy," I warned her, since she deserved to have all the information before she made the attempt. "We did a lot of research on apotheosis last night. The ambrosia works best on people who have divine ancestry, so as a daughter of Zeus, you have that part covered. But the majority of those who drink ambrosia don't survive the process."

"The ambrosia will turn your blood to ichor,"

Danielle added. "Ichor is the blood of the gods. But ichor is toxic to mortals. If the transition to being a god doesn't take, the ichor will still be in your blood, and it will kill you."

"I'm a daughter of Zeus," Rachael reminded us—as if we needed reminding. "Of course the transition to being a god will take. And it's worth the risk. I would rather die than live in the body of a corpse. What kind of life could I possibly have if I stay like this?" She motioned to her monstrous body for emphasis.

"We could try to find another solution," I said. "This might not be the only way."

"But this is the only way for me to become a goddess?" Rachael asked.

"From our research, it seems like it," Danielle said.

"Then I'm doing this." Rachael straightened her shoulders, staring down at the ambrosia. "I *want* to be a goddess. I was brought back from the Underworld, put back into my mutilated corpse, and placed in this cave where the ambrosia can be found. This is my destiny. It *has* to be."

She kneeled down next to the basin, cupped the golden liquid in her hands, and drank it. Then she dipped her hands in again and drank more.

"How much do I need to drink for it to work?" she asked us.

"One cup," Blake said. "At least, that's what it said in the books we read."

She filled her hands twice more with the ambrosia and gulped it down. Then she stood back up, wiping her mouth with the back of her hand. "Was that enough?" she asked.

"We're as new to this as you are," Danielle answered. "I suppose we can wait and—"

She was cut off by Rachael's earsplitting scream.

CHAPTER FOURTEEN

"I t *burns!*" Rachael scratched at her arms, as if she were trying to dig into her flesh and drain out the ambrosia. Chunks of her skin came off with her nails. She held her hands up in front of her face, staring at the shreds of her skin attached to them, and screamed again.

There were gaping holes in her arms where her skin used to be. But it wasn't blood that seeped out of the wounds. It was a thick, glowing, metallic liquid.

Ichor.

The ichor burned through her flesh as it poured out of her body and fell onto the ground, melting her skin and leaving sizzling trails in its wake.

Her screams echoed through the cave, and through her cries, she begged us to help her.

I wanted to run to her and try to heal her, but after my last failed attempt, I knew this would be no different. If the apotheosis process was failing, there was nothing I could do.

Her tears were also made of ichor, and they ran down her face, joining the growing puddle of melted gold on the ground. Her feet melted into the puddle, disappearing until there was nothing left of them anymore. With her feet gone, she fell to her knees, reaching forward to brace herself with her palms and screaming again. Her skin was literally melting off her body now, dripping to the puddle below. The ichor was burning its way through her, leaving nothing in its wake—not even bones.

I watched in horror, hating that there was nothing that I could do to help. All I could do was watch her melt away.

Her final screams echoed through the cave, and then she was silent.

Rachael was gone.

All that remained was a glistening puddle of ichor.

CHAPTER FIFTEEN

W e were all silent, staring at the place where Rachael had been standing. Even though she was gone, I could still hear her awful screams in my mind. The way she'd begged for help. I didn't think I would ever forget her cries for as long as I lived.

"Maybe she'll be okay," Chris finally said, although from the way his voice wavered, I doubted he believed it. "Maybe this is just the first part of the apotheosis process. The ichor is still there. She could rise from it as a goddess..."

"She's not going to rise as a goddess," Blake said, his eyes locked on the puddle that used to be Rachael. "We all saw what just happened to her. The ichor burned through her body. She rejected the transition."

"We can't do that to Kate." Chris's eyes were wide,

locked on the puddle as he backed as far away from it as possible—as if he was afraid that being near it would burn him, too. "What if the same thing happens to her? Hasn't Kate been through enough already? Maybe there's another way… something else we can do to save her…"

"There's no other way," I said. "If there were, Apollo would have told us. And we have to trust that he told us about apotheosis because it's the best and possibly *only* way to get Kate back."

"All Apollo told us was to *learn* about the apotheosis process," Chris said. "He didn't specifically mention ambrosia. And Kate can't even drink the ambrosia! We would have to submerge her in it completely. And we all know from our research that that's never been done before. Maybe we should just go back to the library and try to figure out another option."

"Kate's soul is stuck in the stone," Danielle reminded him, her voice soft. "We know that ambrosia has the power to turn mortals into gods, and the ambrosia is right here in this cave. If the worst happens, and Kate suffers the same fate as Rachael, then at least we'll have freed her soul from the stone. At least she'll be able to find peace. We owe it to her to at least give her that."

"And I don't want to speak badly of the dead, but Kate has a much better chance of surviving the process than Rachael," Blake added. "She has more qualities of a goddess."

"She does," I agreed, although I was glad that Blake had said it first. "We also can't forget that Apollo is the one who recommended this method to us, and he's the god of prophecy. He wouldn't lead us in the wrong direction."

"I know that you're right," Chris said. "It was just—seeing that happen to Rachael... I've seen a lot of scary stuff recently, but that took the cake."

I nodded, since I understood what he meant. I saw a lot of terrifying stuff in Kerberos, but seeing Rachael melt into a puddle of ichor was worse than most of the things I saw while there. The only thing worse had been walking into the cabin and finding Blake's mutilated corpse.

I shivered from thinking about it and stepped closer to Blake, taking his hand in mine. I was more grateful that he was here now than I would ever be able to explain out loud.

"So we're still in agreement?" Danielle asked. "We're moving forward with the process for Kate?"

We didn't get a chance to answer, because a huge orb of fiery light appeared in the middle of a cave, a man materializing in the center. And judging from his angry expression and his eyes that blazed with fire, I doubted he was here to help us.

CHAPTER SIXTEEN

My thoughts shot through my brain at super speed. Apollo traveled through a similar orb of light. But Apollo's orb was yellow, not red. Whoever this was had to be similar to Apollo, and Helios and Apollo were both gods of the sun.

Before the god fully materialized, my hand was on my necklace. I called to Apollo for help, sending him a mental image of the scene in front of me.

The man stepped out of the orb, the light fading behind him. He was tall and muscular, with auburn hair and bronzed skin. Like all the gods, I would have thought he was attractive—if he wasn't looking at us as if he wanted to kill us.

Then the cave glowed with a soft yellow light, lightning cracked down right beside us, a boom that sounded like a bomb exploded, and the smell of sweet perfume drifted through the air. Five gods stood in front of the one who I assumed was Helios—Apollo, Zeus, and three others I hadn't met yet. One was male and two were female. The man had dark hair and dark eyes, and he wore a leather jacket similar to the one Blake always wore. The women looked like total opposites. One resembled a Barbie doll in a tight red dress, stilettos, and her blonde hair styled to perfection. Her eyes were bright blue—nearly the same shade as Danielle's. The other woman was much more low-key in jeans and a t-shirt, her hair held back in a practical ponytail. She wore no makeup, but was still stunningly beautiful.

"Helios." Apollo addressed the god who had appeared in the fiery orb, confirming that my guess about his identity was correct. "You've done quite the job of hiding from us. If you hadn't come here in a rage to kill my daughter and her friends, we might not have found you so quickly."

"I have a right to be here," Helios growled. "Or have you already forgotten about how these four *Elementals* killed one of my immortal cows when they visited my island? Now, to add insult to injury, they destroyed the demigod that I ventured into the Underworld to bring back to Earth. Luck was on my side that Hades was too distracted by the upcoming war to notice, and I was quite proud of my accomplishment. But mortals cannot thwart the gods like that and live to tell the tale."

Zeus stepped forward, each step booming through the cave like thunder. "The demigod you speak of is my daughter," he said. "And since you didn't have Hades's permission to leave with her, you returned her soul to her *corpse*. You made her into an abomination. She may not have survived the apotheosis process, but I'm grateful that her soul has returned to the Underworld, where it belongs."

"The question now is what we're going to do with you." The god in the leather jacket cracked his knuckles and stepped closer to Helios. I assumed he was Ares, the god of war. He held a baseball bat with chains around it, looking at the sun god with rage in his eyes.

Helios grunted, and then his eyes darted around the cave, as if he were trapped.

"Trying to leave?" Zeus laughed and raised an eyebrow, not waiting for Helios to answer. "You won't succeed. I created an electrical shield around the area, blocking your powers and your ability to teleport out of here. You're trapped with us. Which is just our luck, since we were all just meeting on Olympus discussing your fate."

"Don't waste your time." Helios sneered. "Once Typhon rises and the portal is fully open, my fate won't be in your hands for much longer. And no matter how powerful you are, you don't hold the power to seal that portal. If you did, you would have done it already."

"You always were such a pessimist." The goddess who looked like a Barbie frowned and shook her head. "*We* might not be able to close the portal, but the Elementals can. In the past few months, they've proven to be as brave as the most noteworthy heroes to have ever lived. We have faith that they will succeed."

"Oh, Aphrodite." Helios scoffed and crossed his arms. "How about you do what you do best and find another guy to screw, and leave matters of war to the men equipped to handle it. Or is your mind so shallow that you've already forgotten about the war you caused in Troy...?"

"You arrogant fool," Aphrodite snarled back at him. "You'll pay for that." She raised her arms as if preparing to demolish Helios, but Ares wrapped a hand around her wrist, stopping her.

"Wait, my love." He looked at her sternly, and she made no move to try to escape from his hold. In fact, her lips curved upward, as if she enjoyed it. "I'm sure you have a wonderfully torturous plan in mind for Helios, but we *all* want to decide what happens to him. Don't take the thrill of doling out the punishment all for yourself."

"Fine." She huffed, reining her arms back in. "But only because you asked so nicely. *And* I expect you to properly thank me for listening to you when we get back to your bedroom in Olympus." She raised her eyebrows at him, practically purring as she said the last part, and then she kissed him on the mouth—tongue and all.

I looked away from them, wishing they would tone it down a notch. I did *not* need this graphic demonstration of what was going on behind the curtains at Olympus.

"I also want to remind you, Helios, that it's not only the *men* who are equipped to handle battles and war." The goddess in the casual clothing stepped forward, her cool gray eyes daring Helios to contradict her. "Or have you forgotten who you're speaking to?"

"Of course not, Athena," he said her name with a mocking smile. "How could I forget when you're here to remind me?"

"We are in charge of your fate," she said, not miffed by him in the slightest. "It would be in your best interest to grovel at our feet right now—not to irk us further by mocking us to our faces."

"It doesn't matter what I do," Helios said. "Once the Titans rise again, they will free us from your dictatorship at last, and they'll remove whatever punishment you choose to dole out on me."

"Dictatorship?" Apollo repeated, laughing. "Have

you been spending time in Kerberos without telling us? Because you've clearly gone mad."

"That's perfect coming from you," Helios said. "Or have you forgotten that *I* was the god of the sun?" He pointed to himself, the tendons in his neck popping out as he spoke. "I sided with the lot of you during the Second Rebellion, only to have my job taken over and to be reduced to practically nothing!"

"You sided with us to save your own ass." Ares sneered. "Don't think you can convince us otherwise. You should have been grateful that we didn't toss you into Kerberos along with the rest of them, given that you're a Titan yourself."

"We'll figure out a worse punishment for him," Apollo said, turning his gaze to Helios. "You'll regret ever having crossed us by going after our children and our descendants."

"And by trying to assist the Titans in the upcoming battle," Athena added. "Let's not forget about that."

"You all act so high and mighty now," Helios said, glaring at them. "I can't *wait* to see how the Titans punish you after they return. And I can't wait to get my job back, too. I wonder what corner of hell the Titans will send you to once they're back in power? But before they send you off, I'll request for them to let Aphrodite stay behind for a bit, so she can finally kneel down to me and suck my—"

"Enough!" Zeus yelled, bolts of lightning striking the ground around Helios.

Aphrodite's hand was wrapped tightly around Ares's wrist, and if looks could kill, Helios would be dead by now.

After Zeus's outburst, everyone was silent. I looked around at the gods—Zeus, Apollo, Athena, Ares, and Aphrodite—and while I dared not to say it, I was surprised by their behavior. I'd expected them to be more... dignified. Instead, they were bickering like children. Powerful, immortal children.

Apparently, even the gods were far from perfect.

"We're here to determine Helios's fate." Athena was the first to speak up. "As we all know, time is of the essence right now, so we need to stop getting distracted. And since Helios was attempting to kill the mortals in this cave right now—" She paused to glance over at me, Blake, Danielle, and Chris. "Then it's only fitting that they're here to listen to our ideas and let us know which one they prefer."

Ares rolled his eyes, leading me to think he disagreed, but he said nothing.

"Bring it on," Helios said. "Tell me how you plan on punishing me for the next three months. Because that's as long as you have until that portal fully opens again and the Titans return."

"The portal will not be opening, as I have faith that

these mortals will seal it in time," Athena said calmly. "Your punishment will last for as long as we deem fit."

"Precisely." Zeus nodded at Athena, and he stepped in front of the other gods, so he was directly facing Helios. "We are currently undecided between turning you into a human slave for the next century or casting you into the depths of Tartarus. Either punishment would be fitting."

"He should be turned into a human and enslaved to someone who would truly make him pay," Aphrodite mused. "Given his earlier comment to me, I think that making him the consort to an ugly, smelly old hag would be fitting. She'll make him put his mouth where it belongs—twice a day, for the next century." She curved her hand like a cat's and snarled at him, chuckling at her implication. Helios scrunched his nose in disgust.

"That's not a bad suggestion." Zeus nodded and ran his thumb along his jawline. "But what if we turned him into a tree instead? I haven't turned anyone into a tree for a while. Then I could infest the tree with termites, and they would consume the bark for the next century, making sure Helios feels the pain of being slowly eaten alive..." He smiled, clearly proud of himself for coming up with such a plan. "I like that idea," he said brightly, turning to the other gods. "Should I do it?"

"From experience, I can vouch that being turned

into a human is the worst punishment possible," Apollo said. "I'm with Aphrodite on this one. Although, I think he should be made ugly and weak, and forced to do hard labor in the burning sun for the next century."

"You're all wrong," Ares growled. "We should throw him into Tartarus and get it over with. Nothing's worse than the pit of Tartarus itself."

"Except for Kerberos," Athena reminded him. "But since gods cannot travel through the portal until it's fully opened—and we have to hope that circumstances will never reach that point—Tartarus is our best option. However," she continued, holding her hand up so the other gods didn't interrupt her. "Since we all have varying opinions on what should be done to Helios, and since Helios has caused so much trouble for the Elementals, I think it would be fitting for Nicole—as the only demigod of their group—to decide his fate."

CHAPTER SEVENTEEN

"M e?" I swallowed, unsure that I'd heard her right. "You want *me* to decide how to punish a god?"

"I think that it would be fitting," Athena said. "You heard all of our ideas. You can choose the punishment that you feel would best make Helios pay for his crimes, or suggest one of your own."

"I don't even get a fair trial on Olympus?" Helios asked. "Instead, I get only five of the twelve Olympians, and this *mortal* will decide my fate?" He spat out the word "mortal" as if it were the equivalent to vermin.

A lightning bolt cracked down next to Zeus, and he gripped it in his hand. "The other Olympians are dealing with issues caused by the weakening portal and the threat of the Titans' return." His anger pulsated through the bolt of lightning and flashed through the cave. "I am King of the gods, so what I say is what will happen. And I say that the mortal will decide your fate, as long as the other gods here and I agree that her decision is an appropriate punishment." He turned to me, and despite how intimidating he was with the lightning bolt, I stood strong under his gaze. "What have you decided?" he asked.

"I would like to discuss this with the other Elementals," I said. "If you don't mind."

"Wise girl," Athena said, and Apollo smiled, as if proud that I was his daughter. "Of course you should discuss your decision with them, but we have a limited amount of time, so make haste."

I nodded and glanced at the others, nervous and unsure where to begin. It didn't help that the Olympians were watching. "Can we discuss this alone?" I asked. "Please?"

"I will create a diplomatic dome for you," Athena agreed. "You will have complete privacy when inside— no one will be able to hear or see you. The dome will remain intact for ten minutes. Afterward, you will emerge and inform us of your decision."

She waved her hand, and a building that resembled a large igloo appeared nearby—except instead of being made of ice, it was a solid, metallic material. We walked through the doorway, and once the last one of us was through, it sealed behind us. The inside of the sphere was cloudy and perfectly smooth—it was like we were inside an opaque, human-sized snow globe. Curious, I pressed a hand against the wall. It was sturdy and cool to the touch, like glass.

Could the gods *really* not hear us when we were inside here? There was no way to know for sure, but since we didn't have another option, we would have to trust them.

"We should get on with this, since we don't have much time," I said, looking around at each of them. "What are you all thinking?"

"We should throw Helios into Tartarus," Blake spoke up first. "It's the worst part of the Underworld, and once he's trapped down there, we'll be rid of him for the rest of our lives. He'll never give us another problem again."

"I liked Zeus's idea," Chris chimed in. "Turning him into a tree and infesting the tree with termites. But really, I'm fine with any of the options."

"I vote human," Danielle said. "Aphrodite's idea about forcing him to be a male consort *was* pretty amusing."

I couldn't help noticing that they were each supporting the punishment proposed by their godly ancestor. Especially because I was about to do the same.

Sort of. I planned on putting my own spin on the punishment, too.

"I also think that Helios should be turned into a human," I said, glancing at Danielle to acknowledge that I agreed with the first part of her plan. "But only *after* we seal the portal to Kerberos. He's too dangerous to have around before the portal is sealed, especially as a human, since then he could stroll right into Kerberos and make a deal with the Titans. So I'm thinking we should throw him into Tartarus, but only temporarily. Once we've sealed the portal, I would like to have him brought back to Earth as a human for a century. But instead of being bound in servitude to a stranger, I want him bound in servitude to us—the Elementals."

"I like it," Blake said, smiling. "I'm behind you one hundred percent."

"I'm impressed," Danielle chimed in. "It's a better idea than any of the gods had."

"Thanks," I said, taking a second to let it sink in that Danielle had complimented me. "But we should be humble about it when we tell them our decision. We don't want to risk accidentally insulting them by not choosing one of their ideas."

"They asked for your opinion," Chris reminded me. "And your decision is pretty kick-ass, if you ask me. It'll be fun to boss Helios around for the next century."

"We're all in agreement?" I asked.

They all said yes, and I breathed easier, glad I had their support.

"Okay." I stood straighter and walked to where the door to the dome had been. "Let's tell the gods what we decided."

CHAPTER EIGHTEEN

"I like it," Zeus said after we told him our idea for Helios's punishment. "But there's one major problem with it."

"What's that?" I asked.

"Helios's punishment is to last for an entire century. As mortals, it's unlikely that any of you will live for that long."

I frowned, since I hadn't thought about that. It was a good point. And I had no idea what the solution could be.

"We located the ambrosia for a reason," Danielle chimed in. "We want to transform Kate into a goddess. If it works, Kate will be immortal, and she can be Helios's master after the rest of us have passed away."

"Very well." Athena nodded. "And if Kate's apotheosis is unsuccessful, what will become of Helios then?"

"I hope it works," I said. "But if it doesn't, perhaps it's best to keep Helios in Tartarus."

"So, Apollo's spawn has some sense after all," Ares said.

"I accept your proposition." Zeus waved his hand, and a lightning bolt struck Helios.

Helios screamed, his body lit up and buzzing with electricity. Then he was gone. All that remained was a charred spot on the ground where he'd been standing, and the smell of burnt flesh lingering in the air.

"Did you just disintegrate Helios?" Chris asked, his eyes wide.

"No, I didn't disintegrate anything." Zeus chuckled. "I can assure you that Helios is completely intact. I sent him straight to Tartarus, which is where he'll remain until we know the results of Kate's apotheosis, and the portal to Kerberos is sealed."

"No pressure or anything," Chris muttered.

"You've done well so far," Athena said. "Especially since you had some added help from the gods." She glanced at Zeus and Apollo after saying that part—she didn't look thrilled that they'd helped us, but she didn't seem angry about it, either. "And I'm grateful that you're going forth with Kate's apotheosis. As her godly ancestor, you have my blessing with the process."

"Does that mean the apotheosis will definitely be successful?" I asked.

"There are some things in this universe that not even the gods can control," Athena said. "Especially since apotheosis has never been attempted on someone in Kate's... condition. But with the gods on her side, the chance of it being successful is far more likely."

"Thank you." I lowered my head in respect. "It means a lot."

"And now, we must be on our way," Apollo said. "Remember—even though we won't be with you physically, we believe in you. The primordial deities wouldn't have given you your powers if you didn't have what it takes to save the world."

And then, as quickly as they'd appeared, the five Olympian gods were gone.

CHAPTER NINETEEN

We left the cave and called Hypatia, who created a portal for us back to Darius's house. We caught them up on everything that had happened in the cave, and collected the statue of Kate from where we'd been keeping it in the basement.

Looking at Kate in her current condition never got easier. Her hands were raised in front of her, as if she was trying to hide from Medusa's gaze. Her eyes were wide—terrified—and her mouth was open in mid-scream. Her entire face was twisted in torment. I hoped that her last moment hadn't been painful, but looking at the statue, it was impossible to convince myself that that was the case.

Chris used his power to float Kate's statue onto a

rolling platform. Then Hypatia created a portal to the cave, and we all went through, bringing Kate with us.

I'd expected the golden puddle of ichor—all that remained of Rachael—to still be there. But it was gone. Hopefully Hades had chosen to send her soul to Elysium—the section of the Underworld most similar to Heaven.

Darius stepped up to the basin, studying the golden liquid inside. "Incredible," he said, his eyes lighting up as he took it in. "In all my years, I never once dreamed that I would actually see ambrosia—the nectar of the gods."

"Don't get too close," I warned him. "I doubt any of us would fall in, but after what happened to Rachael... we can't be too careful." I shuddered, slammed again by the memory of Rachael melting from the inside out.

"We must be deep in the Cave of Antiparos," Hypatia observed, looking around. "The cave is open to tourists, and has been explored since the time of the ancients. But this section of it is untouched by mortals."

"There's much more to the cave than this," I added. "When we first found it, it was through a different portal—one in the woods close to the school. We had to figure our way down a hundred foot cliff and across a lake of boiling water—all so we could find the Book of Shadows, which was waiting for us in this room."

It was hard to believe that had only been a few months ago. We'd been through so much since then that it felt like so much longer. Back then, I was so inexperienced with my powers. It was crazy to think about how far I'd come—how far we *all* had come.

"Even in those other sections, the cave showed no signs of anyone else having been there," Danielle pointed out. "The articles I found online about the Cave of Antiparos said that it had been fully explored. So the parts of the cave that we've seen must be hidden to humans."

"That would make sense," Jason said. "I'm sure the gods didn't want humans stumbling upon the portal to Kerberos. But we don't have time to further investigate that right now. Because we're here for one reason—to save Kate."

"Yes," I said, glancing back over at the statue of my friend. I hoped beyond all hope that this would work. Despite Kate's fate with Medusa, I never accepted that she was gone, and I didn't think the others had, either. Now was the time of truth. If the apotheosis didn't work, we would have to face the fact that Kate was gone forever.

I was hopeful, excited, and terrified at the same time.

"Before we start, I would like us to do a meditation,"

Darius said. "As you know, green energy represents success and luck. I think we can all agree that those are things that Kate could benefit from right now. So let's gather around her statue, hold hands, and direct green energy toward her."

We formed a circle around her—Blake on one side of me, Danielle on the other. I grabbed both of their hands and closed my eyes, reminded of a similar exercise we did months ago, when we meditated under the Olympian Comet. I never could have guessed that that one night would have been so pivotal.

Back then, my biggest concerns had been getting the top spot on the tennis team and wondering if my crush returned my feelings. I'd never seen death, and I certainly never thought that I would ever kill a living creature. Now, so much had changed. I'd fought and killed to save the lives of people I loved. I'd seen people die. I'd been given so much responsibility, and I had the weight of the world on my shoulders. If we failed at this quest, the world as I knew it wouldn't exist anymore.

But I couldn't let myself think about that right now. Because right now there was only one thing I needed to focus on—making sure Kate's apotheosis went as smoothly as possible.

I cleared my mind and focused on green energy, feeling its presence rolling over my skin and pulling it into my body. It filled me, bright and warm, and I gathered it until it felt like it was about to burst out of me.

Then, unable to contain it anymore, I sent all of it out toward Kate.

CHAPTER TWENTY

O nce finished, I opened my eyes, and we let go of each other's hands.

"It's time to begin the apotheosis." Hypatia swallowed—I could tell she was nervous—and her gaze was fixed on Kate.

Chris raised his arms, using his power to levitate Kate's statue and fly it over to the basin until it hovered over the ambrosia. "Are you all ready?" he asked.

I reached for Blake's hand, nervous about what was going to happen next. This was the moment of truth. If everything went well, Kate would be with us again.

If everything didn't go well... I refused to think about that unless it happened. This *had* to work. The gods wouldn't have led us in this direction otherwise.

"We're ready," Danielle said, and I echoed her sentiment along with the others.

I didn't truly think there was ever a way to feel ready for something like this, but we were as close as we would ever be.

Slowly, Chris lowered the statue of Kate into the ambrosia. First her feet, then her legs, her body, and her head, until she was gone—submerged completely below the liquid.

I held my breath, making my way over to the basin to peer over the edge. The surface of the ambrosia was flat—there was no clue that the statue of Kate was in there. It was so flat that I could see my reflection in it.

Then it started to bubble—small bubbles, as if simmering to a boil. The bubbles were directly over the place where we'd lowered Kate into the liquid. The bubbles grew and grew until it looked like the ambrosia was boiling completely.

I clenched my fists, looking down at the ambrosia in fear. What if Kate was down there melting, like what had happened to Rachael? If that's what was happening to her, how would we even know? The ambrosia was the same color as the ichor—gold. Kate could be drowning and terrified and have no idea where she was or what was happening.

She could be dying painfully, and she would be alone.

"We have to help her." I jerked my head up to look at Chris and pointed at the ambrosia. "Pull her out of there! Now!"

Chris held his hands out, as if about to do it, but he hesitated. "What if it's working?" he asked. "What if that's happening because Kate's transitioning into a goddess?"

"The process has already started," Blake said, confident and strong. "If it's not working... there won't be anything we can do for her at this point. We have to wait and hope for the best."

I nodded, since I knew he was right. It was just torture, standing here and waiting, not knowing what was happening to Kate beneath the ambrosia.

Maybe nothing was actually happening at all. Maybe our idea to dunk the statue of Kate in the ambrosia was stupid. Because as far as we knew, the ambrosia had to be *drunk* to take effect. We'd been hoping that by dunking her, it would absorb into her body, but since this had never been done before there was no way to know for sure.

Then there was a rumbling from deep in the basin, and a shadow crept up to the surface. Kate. She rose slowly—first the top of her head, and the rest of her followed.

The ambrosia rolled off of her, like oil on water, revealing a version of Kate that was more beautiful than ever before. She wasn't stone anymore. She looked different than I remembered her, but she was *alive*.

I stared at her, taking in her changed appearance. Her previously freckled skin was now smooth and flawless. Her hair blew around her face, its previous ash brown color now tinted with a stunning auburn. Her green eyes sparkled more than ever, as if made of actual emeralds. She wore the same green dress that she'd worn when we fought Medusa, and it billowed around her, making her look like a piece of artwork come to life.

She hovered atop the golden liquid and slowly floated forward, her feet landing gently on the ground. She blinked and looked at each of us, her expression a mix of confusion and awe.

"Kate?" I said her name softly. "It's really you?"

"Yes." Her voice was more melodic than ever, and she raised her hands in front of her, flexing them and examining them. "What's going on?" She sounded dazed, and she looked back up at us, her eyes sparkling with confusion. "What happened to me?"

"It's a long story." Chris beamed and ran up to her, wrapping his arms around her in a huge hug. He finally pulled away, the grin still on his face, and said, "But we're glad to have you back."

CHAPTER TWENTY-ONE

J ason created a portal for us back to Darius's house, and once there, Kate changed out of her fancy dress and into jeans and a t-shirt that she had in the basement for training. She looked more normal in regular clothing, but there was still an ethereal glow around her that made it clear that she was different—that reminded us that she was now a *goddess*.

Once we'd all freshened up, we sat down in the living room and caught Kate up on everything that had happened since Medusa had turned her to stone.

"Thank you for saving me," she said once we were finished. "But... you performed the apotheosis process without a god present at the ceremony?"

"The gods were there *before* the ceremony," I

reminded her. "When they gave Helios his punishment. Once Helios was taken care of, they gave us their blessing and left to deal with other matters."

"Hm." Kate gazed out the window, appearing deep in thought.

"How does it feel to be a goddess?" Chris asked her, pulling her attention back to us. "Do you feel different? You definitely *look* different. In a good way, of course." He smiled, a tint of red crawling up his neck and reaching his cheeks.

"I don't feel *too* much different," she said, holding her arms out in front of her and examining them. "I seem to have the same level of control over my element that I did when I was mortal. But I *am* worried that a god wasn't present during the ceremony." She chewed on her lower lip, her eyes full of worry. "Stealing ambrosia to turn someone into a goddess without another god present is a hugely punishable offense. I know the gods are busy right now with the threat of Typhon and the Titans on the horizon, but once they figure out what I am now..." She shuddered, sheer terror on her smooth features. "I'm scared about what they might decide to do with me."

"Athena gave us her blessing," I reminded her, resting my hand on hers in an attempt to calm her down. "She wouldn't have given her blessing if she meant to punish us for following through without another god there with us."

Then the air next to Kate shimmered, and someone appeared on the couch next to her—Athena. She wore the same jeans and t-shirt as earlier, and besides her gray eyes, it was easy to tell that she and Kate were related.

"Athena?" Kate spoke her name, her mouth open in shock.

"Yes." The gray-eyed goddess nodded and scooted closer to her. "I'm so thrilled to see that the apotheosis was successful."

"You mean you're not mad?" Kate asked. "You're not going to punish us for going through with the process without a god by our side?"

"I couldn't do that, since you *did* have a god by your side the entire time," she said, smiling mischievously. "I was there with you in that cave, although I hid myself from sight. After all, I gave my blessing. And while I doubted anything would go wrong, not many survive the apotheosis process, so I wanted to be there just in case you needed my assistance. Luckily, it succeeded on its own. Congratulations."

"Wow... thank you," Kate said, and then she looked around at all of us. "And thank you all so much for doing this for me. That time spent trapped inside the stone..." She shivered, as if the memories chilled her to the bone. "I was conscious the whole time I was in there, but I couldn't see or hear anything, and I couldn't move. I was terrified that I would be stuck like that forever. I know I was only in there for a few days, but it felt like an eternity…"

"Well, you're back with us now," Chris said. "That's what matters."

"Yes," Kate agreed. "When I was trapped in there, I wished that someone would shatter my statue, to set my soul free. I wonder if that would have worked? Or would I have just been trapped in the pieces forever?"

"Shattering Medusa's statues will not free the souls," Athena confirmed. "If that happens, the soul would be shattered as well. And while no soul can ever be gone forever, being shattered into pieces is as close to permanently gone as possible."

"The only way to free the soul is by submerging the stone in the ambrosia?" Danielle asked.

"Yes," Athena said. "Although, Kate's case was a rare one. For the majority—if not all—of Medusa's statues, the apotheosis process would kill them."

"But their souls would be brought to the Under-world," Kate said. "Correct?"

"That's correct." Athena nodded.

"Then after we defeat Typhon and stop the Titans, I'm going to make it my personal mission to free all the souls that Medusa's trapped." Kate straightened, her eyes gleaming with determination. "With your permission, of course. I understand that their apotheosis won't be successful, but they deserve to be free to go to the Underworld."

"I'll help you," I said, and the others chimed in that they would help as well.

"I think that sounds like a fantastic plan, and I gladly give my blessing," Athena said. "But on the note of Typhon, I think it's time that I take my leave. After all, you don't have much longer until he rises from Mount Etna."

"Five days," Blake said. "That's all the time we have until the spring equinox."

"Not very long at all," Athena said. "But the five of you are more than capable. I haven't witnessed heroes like you since the days of Hercules and Jason."

"Thank you," Kate said. "Being compared to the great heroes of the ancient times—I never dreamed anyone would say that about me. It means a lot. But... before you leave, I do have one more question."

Athena said nothing, simply nodding for Kate to continue.

"What should I expect now that I'm a goddess?" she asked. "I've tested out my powers, and they don't feel any different. I can still access my element, but not any stronger than I could before."

"That's to be expected, since the apotheosis process

turns mortals into minor goddesses," Athena explained. "You will never be nearly as powerful as myself or the other Olympians—or the Titans, for that matter—who were all born from two godly parents. You will, however, have the same powers that you did while you were mortal, along with immortality and eternal youth. And since you're a descendant of mine this probably doesn't need saying, but I hope you use this gift wisely."

"I will," Kate said. "I promise."

"Also, every god has something they stand for—something they represent and lead over," Athena added. "For me, that's wisdom and battle strategy. Aphrodite is the goddess of love, Ares is the god of war, Hades is the god of the Underworld, and so forth. Now that you've been given this gift, it's your responsibility to choose one original cause to take under your wing and make your own."

"Do I need to choose now?" Kate asked. "Because I would like some time to think about it…"

"You do not need to choose immediately." Athena placed her hand on Kate's shoulder, the gesture motherly and kind. "Just keep the thought in the back of your mind, as the sooner you choose, the better."

"Understood," Kate said, her eyes serious.

"But I know you have more pressing matters to worry about right now—such as Typhon—so it's truly time for me to leave." Athena stood up and studied each of us, as if sizing up if we were ready for what was coming. "I give you my blessing in the trials ahead, and wish you the best of luck."

Her body shimmered, slowly fading from view, and then she was gone.

CHAPTER TWENTY-TWO

The next few days were spent training, vanquishing creatures that came through the portal, and strategizing for the upcoming fight with Typhon. School had been put on the back burner. After missing so many days, I would most likely have to go to summer school, but I would deal with that when it came to it.

What little free time I had was spent with my family, catching them up on what had happened in my absence and assuring them that we had this under control. As always, I left out the scariest parts of the story when I caught them up, as I didn't want to worry them any more than necessary. All that mattered was that we would succeed, and they and everyone else in the world would be safe.

And if the worst happened and we *didn't* succeed... hopefully the end of the world would come so quickly that no one would know any differently.

We were finishing up training on Friday when Darius received a 911 call from Jason, who was guarding the area around the portal. The witch who had been guarding when the giants escaped had never been found, and by this point, he was presumed dead. So witches were no longer being put on guard. That job was being handled by Head Elders, who were taking turns portaling to Kinsley to work their shifts.

"A pack of dragons escaped from Kerberos," Darius warned us after getting off the phone. "Gather the weapons you need, and *hurry*."

We did as he said, but when we portaled to the playground, the dragons were too far away for our powers to reach them. And from their bright orange color, there was no mistaking what breed these dragons were—Helios's solar dragons. They looked the same as the ones we'd come across in Kerberos, the ones that had given us rides to the top of the mountain in exchange for the Golden Sword of Athena. Perhaps they *were* the same ones.

The solar dragons were an enigma—while they were under Helios's command, they seemed to think for themselves and not be on any one side. Now that Helios was banished, he wouldn't have even a semblance of control over them. There was no saying *what* they would do now or whose side they were on.

Even though it was a long shot, I strung an arrow through my bow and aimed at the dragon in the back of the pack. But it was too late. The dragons flew at supernatural speed, and they were already out of range. The arrow missed, and the dragons flew into the night, disappearing over the horizon.

"They're flying east," Danielle said, staring out at where they'd disappeared.

"Mount Etna is east," Blake said. "It can't be a coincidence that they're heading that way."

"Greece is east as well," Chris pointed out. "Maybe they're just flying home."

"What'll happen when the humans see them?" I asked. "Won't they freak out?"

"Unless they come into direct physical contact with them, they won't be able to see them," Blake explained. "Their minds can't process magic like ours can. *We* can see the dragons… but a human would probably just think they were seeing large birds."

"So Becca was only able to see the true form of the harpy because the harpy touched her," I realized.

"Yes." Kate nodded, gazing off into the sky. "And with so many creatures escaping, there will be more of them on Earth than there have been in thousands of years. Even if we succeed in stopping Typhon and the Titans... after this, the world will never be the same."

CHAPTER TWENTY-THREE

Before I knew it, we were standing in Darius's living room, in our gear and with our weapons, waiting for Hypatia to create the portal to Mount Etna. She'd been in Italy for a few days, making sure everything was prepared for our arrival. I paced around, unable to stay still as I went over the plan in my mind. I *wanted* to feel ready, but I didn't. How could I ever feel ready for something like this?

We'd been doing meditation exercises for the past hour, focusing on yellow and orange energy—focus and strength—to prepare us for the upcoming fight. I'd also been calling upon blue energy to help calm down. It helped, but I still felt jittery. After all, most of the other times we'd gone off into a big fight—like when we left for Greece, Antarctica, and Kerberos—we'd been thrown into it without having much time to worry. The only other time we'd had time to train and prepare was for Medusa.

Typhon was going to make the fight with Medusa look *easy*.

The only thing keeping me from completely freaking out was the knowledge that out of all the witches—and demigods—in the world, *we* were the ones chosen by the gods to complete this task. They wouldn't have selected us if they didn't believe we were capable of succeeding.

If the gods believed in us, then I had to believe in us, too.

"You okay?" Blake walked up to me and took both of my hands in his. The moment he did, calmness rushed through my veins—blue energy. Instead of using the blue energy to calm himself down, Blake had sent it to me.

"Thanks," I told him, giving his hands a small squeeze. "You didn't have to do that. I'm sure you need the blue energy for yourself."

"You needed it more than me," he insisted. "I know you might not admit it, but I could tell."

I nodded, because he was right. Then I gathered red energy—courage and love—and sent it toward him. He held my hands tighter, his gaze intense, and sent me back red energy in return.

We would all make it through this. We *had* to. I'd already lost Blake once—I couldn't lose him again.

But I couldn't push down the knowledge that there was a chance we wouldn't make it. Despite our powers, we weren't immune to death. Except for Kate, of course, since she was now immortal.

Darius's phone rang, and my heart pounded faster, knowing it had to be Hypatia.

"She's ready to create the portal," Darius said after hanging up.

I nodded, and Blake and I made our way to the center of the room to join the others. Kate held onto the backpack with Medusa's head. As the only immortal in the group, it was safest for her to be in charge of it. She and Chris were holding hands, and Danielle stood as strong as ever—a warrior princess ready to fight.

"You all know the plan." Darius looked around at each of us, his eyes brimming with concern. "I've trained you the best that I can in the time we've been allowed. You've fought some of the most dangerous monsters in history, and while you may not have killed all of them, you've managed to survive. The five of you are the strongest willed and most resilient people I've ever known, and I'm honored to be your teacher. So go out there today knowing that you're trained and ready, and make me proud."

"We will," Chris said, his voice strong and confident. "We're the Elementals. You can count on us—always."

Then Hypatia created the portal, and together, the five of us stepped through.

CHAPTER TWENTY-FOUR

The end of the world looked like it had already hit the island of Sicily, Italy. The sun hadn't risen yet, but I could still make out the volcano looming out in the distance, gray clouds and ash pouring from the crater and emptying out into the sky. We'd portaled straight onto a helicopter tarmac, where one helicopter waited for us, along with a pilot. I recognized the pilot as one of the witches who had been on the crew of the yacht in Greece.

"Ash has been rising from the volcano for the past week," Hypatia informed us. "Geologists are baffled. But I think it's safe to say that if Typhon frees himself from the volcano, this disaster will be worse than when Poseidon lost his temper in 1906 and caused the Great

San Francisco Earthquake. If Typhon fully escapes, this entire island could be blown to pieces."

"We'll stop him before it gets that far," Blake said.

"Exactly." Kate nodded. "The first thing he'll see when his head emerges from that crater will be Medusa's gaze."

"And the moment Typhon's finished off, I'll create a portal large enough for the helicopter to fly through and bring us back to Kinsley," Hypatia said.

"I still don't like that you're risking yourself by coming with us," I told her. "I know we need a Head Elder with us to create the portal home since it's the only way to know our exact location once the fight is over, but can't it be someone else? I don't understand why it has to be *you*."

I'd been worried about Hypatia coming with us since she'd first told us about that part of the plan days ago. Yes, she was a Head Elder, which made her powerful, but she didn't have *close* to the amount of power that the five of us Elementals had. She wouldn't be able to do much of anything in the fight against Typhon—if it came to a fight at all. She was just another person who I'd come to care about who would be risking her life for us.

"If not me, then who else?" she asked. "I've been with the five of you since you journeyed through Greece to slay the hydra. I know what the five of you can do—I've seen it first hand—and I believe in you. I'm proud to accompany you on this mission."

"Thank you," I told her, since she clearly wasn't budging on this. "We won't let you down."

But even as I said the words, I wished I could believe that everything would go as planned as much as everyone else. How were they so confident when I felt like a wreck inside?

"Um, you guys?" the helicopter pilot said, pointing up at the sky. "Are those what I think they are? Because if they are… then we're in big trouble."

I turned around to look where he was pointing, and saw six orange dragons flying through the sky, heading straight in our direction.

Crap, I thought, panic rising in my throat as they got closer.

This was *not* in our plan of how things were supposed to go this morning.

CHAPTER TWENTY-FIVE

Kate reached for her bag. "Get ready to close your eyes," she warned. "Because I'm turning these dragons to stone."

"Wait!" I reached forward, stopping her from unzipping the bag.

Her eyes widened, and she looked at me like I was crazy. But she didn't try to push me aside, which I assumed meant she was willing to listen.

"We've worked with these dragons before." I spoke quickly, since the dragons were getting closer. "I know that they're *Helios's* Solar Dragons, but their only loyalty is to themselves. If we can offer them something they want, they might help us in this fight."

"I already gave them my sword once." Danielle held

the Golden Sword in the air, ready to fight. "I'm *not* giving it up again."

"Then what are we offering them?" Chris asked. "We need to think quick, because they're almost here."

"We'll figure it out," I said. "For now, let's see if they would be willing to make a deal and side with *us* against Typhon."

"We also need to be ready to fight, just in case." Blake held his lighter in one hand, and his sword in the other. "At least this time, I'm here to protect you from their fire."

I nodded, since I knew he said that to be comforting —and that his power *could* save us if the dragons attacked—but I hated the thought of him using up energy before the fight with Typhon. Hopefully it wouldn't come to that.

"And I've got Medusa's head ready to whip out the *moment* the dragons make it clear they're not cooperating," Kate said. "But you're right. The more numbers we have on our side against Typhon, the better. Plus, if these dragons have any sense of self-preservation—and from what you've told me about your previous encounter with them, they do—it's in their best interest to side with us."

"They *will* side with us," I said, trying to convince myself as much as the others. Because while I believed we had a chance, they were also *dragons*. Could any of us truly know what they would do?

"Hold down your weapons so they know we don't want to fight." Kate stepped forward, the wind whipping around her hair as she stared out at the approaching dragons. "But still be on guard and ready to use them if necessary."

I did as she said and lowered my bow to my side. The others did the same with their weapons.

"We don't want to fight you!" I yelled once they were within hearing range.

They stopped flying toward us, and they flapped their wings to fly in place overhead.

I assumed that meant they were listening. "We've worked with you before," I continued, speaking loudly to project my voice. "It happened in another timeline, so you won't remember it, but you accepted a deal from us in exchange for your help. I think we can work out another deal today, if you'll give us a chance and hear us out."

They looked to the largest dragon in the front of their formation—I assumed he was their leader. I held my breath in anticipation. This was a huge risk, because we couldn't afford to weaken our energy by using our powers right now. But if the dragons chose to attack, we would have no choice but to fight back.

Luckily, the leader lowered himself to the ground

and shifted to his human form. Tall, strong, and pale, with bright auburn hair, I recognized him from the first time I met him in Kerberos. But of course he didn't recognize me, since the timeline when we'd met had been erased.

The others in the pack followed his lead and shifted into their human forms. They all had similar skin and hair colors, and like before, they were all naked. I supposed it didn't make sense for them to bother with clothes, since they would rip them apart every time they shifted.

"The only way you could remember another timeline is if Chronos allowed you to travel through a time portal," the dragon leader finally spoke, his voice low and steady. "He did this for you?"

"Yes." I nodded. "The primordial deities want us to succeed in defeating Typhon and sealing the portal to Kerberos. We failed in the original timeline, but since the primordial deities are on our side, Chronos allowed Danielle and me to travel through a time portal to correct our mistakes. There's no time right now to get into specifics, but I hope you take my word that in the previous timeline, we worked out a deal and you helped us on our quest. We hope you'll be able to agree to another deal with us today."

"Especially since Helios has been banished to

Tartarus, so you're now free to act independently from him," Kate chimed in.

"We are dragons," the leader reminded us, although we hardly needed reminding. "Yes, we drove Helios's chariot around the sun and worked out many mutually beneficial deals with him, but we *always* act independently and in our best interests. The Olympians should have known that about us before banishing us to Kerberos with the rest of the creatures who sided against them in the Second Rebellion."

"They should have," Danielle agreed. "But we all know that the Olympians are far from perfect, and they *and* the primordial deities are on our side in this war. We're going to win. And if you help us today, they'll be forced to take notice, and you'll be rewarded for your bravery."

"Rewarded how?" The leader's mate stepped forward and raised an eyebrow. "Are you making us an offer?"

"Yes." I stepped forward as well, crossing my fingers that this would work. "If you help us fight Typhon today and do not turn on us afterward, we promise you protection by the Twelve Olympians. You will be forgiven for your previous crimes against them, and once this war is over, you'll get a clean slate."

"Who are you to make such a lofty promise?" the pack leader asked. "I don't see any Olympians here with you today. How can we know that this deal will be kept?"

"I am Nicole Cassidy, daughter of the god Apollo, and gifted with power over the element of spirit." I raised my head high, standing strong and holding my gaze with his. "And I swear on Zeus that the gods will cooperate with this agreement."

"No." Hypatia gasped. "If the gods don't accept, Zeus will be forced to kill you."

"I know," I said. "But it won't come to that, because they *will* accept."

But as confident as I was trying to sound, I couldn't be one hundred percent sure. It was simply a risk I needed to take. The first rays of sunlight were appearing over the horizon, and more ash was rising from the volcano by the second. We didn't have enough time to figure out what else the dragons would be willing to trade.

In Kerberos, Erebus had warned us that dragons were selfish creatures who would only help others if it benefitted them. I knew in my gut that this—guaranteed safety—was of utmost value to them. Plus, they would attack us if we didn't strike a deal with them. Medusa's head could only turn them to stone one at a time, which would give them a chance to do some serious damage to us. Our chance of surviving a fight with six dragons and then having enough energy to win in the fight against Typhon was slim to none.

So basically, we were dead if they didn't accept the offer. I only *might* be dead if they did accept the offer. Hopefully the gods would go along with the terms. If they refused—and I couldn't imagine why they would refuse, since these terms could save the world—I hoped that Apollo would go to bat for me and convince them to change their minds.

"I also swear on Zeus that if you help us defeat Typhon, you'll be safe after the war," Blake said, stepping up to stand next to me. He nodded at me once, as if telling me not to stop him from doing this. But I didn't plan on it, so I took his hand and squeezed it, hoping he got the message that I appreciated his support.

"I swear on Zeus, too," Kate said, and soon she was followed by Danielle, Chris, Hypatia, and even the helicopter pilot.

"We're all willing to risk our lives to ensure your safety," I told the dragons, more confident now that I had the support of the others. "When we win, we're going to be on the *right* side of history, and we're offering you a spot there with us. But we don't have much time before the equinox, so we need an answer. Will you accept our offer and fight with us against Typhon? Will you be a part of saving the world?"

CHAPTER TWENTY-SIX

They didn't answer for a few seconds, and I stood frozen in fear, terrified that they would refuse.

"We accept," the leader finally said.

I let out a long breath of relief, able to move again. It worked. The dragons were going to fight with us. We still had a lot to work out from here—such as hoping the gods followed through on their end of the bargain, but at least it was a good first step.

"That was easier than I thought it would be." Kate lowered her hand from the bag, clearly accepting that she wouldn't need to use Medusa's head on the dragons, although she did look perplexed.

"You have Chronos on your side," the dragon leader explained. "If we refused you, what would stop him from creating another time portal and sending you back through it to attack us the moment we escaped from Kerberos? It's a risk we cannot take. Plus," he continued, a smirk crossing his face. "We never came here to hurt you. We always intended on helping you, so you would not force us back into that dreadful hell dimension. You only sweetened the deal by promising amnesty from the gods."

"What?" My mouth dropped open, shocked. "Seriously?"

"Yes," he said, his eyes twinkling in amusement. "Seriously." Then he stepped up to the helicopter and shook his head. "Although I must say, your choice of transportation leaves much to be desired. If Typhon gets one of his hands around this clunky metal flying contraption, he will crush it in his fists."

"Then we'll have to make sure he doesn't get his hands on it, because it's the only mode of transportation that we have," Blake said. "We don't have time to find anything else."

"You may not," the female dragon said. "But we do." She put her fingers between her lips and whistled, and before I could blink, a golden chariot zoomed over the horizon and landed softly on the tarmac. "Helios's golden chariot, at your service." She dramatically motioned toward it as if she were the fairy godmother who'd transformed a pumpkin into a carriage so Cinderella could get to the ball. "It's indestructible—not even the rays of the sun can melt it. And we will fly it for you, of course."

"But can we all fit in it?" Chris asked. "It only looks large enough for one person."

"The chariot will adjust in size to however many people it needs to carry," she explained. "Step on board and see for yourself."

Chris's eyes bugged out—apparently he thought that was the coolest thing ever—and he rushed on board. Kate followed him, and just like the dragon promised, the chariot stretched and grew to accommodate her. It did the same when Danielle stepped on, too.

"How indestructible is this thing?" Danielle raised the Golden Sword, and before I could scream for her to stop, she swung it down onto the edge of the chariot. It clanged against the metal, and she pulled the sword back to her side, examining the damage on the chariot. "No dent," she confirmed. "The chariot can't be destroyed, even by the Golden Sword of Athena."

"That's the true Golden Sword of Athena?" the dragon leader stared at it, practically salivating at the sight.

"Don't even think about it." Danielle scowled and pulled the sword closer. "This sword is mine, and it's staying that way."

I smiled, glad that in this timeline, Danielle didn't have to give up the sword to the dragons.

"After you?" Blake said, motioning for me to get on board the chariot next.

I hopped onto the platform, and he held my hand, helping me. The moment I stepped on, the floor stretched again, and there was enough room for me to stand on it along with the others. I ran my fingers over the golden ledge of the chariot, marveling in the details of the carving. The vehicle was truly exquisite. Blake jumped on to join us, and it stretched out again to accommodate him.

"With the dragons flying the chariot, I suppose you don't have any use for me now?" the helicopter pilot asked.

"I will create a portal home for you," Hypatia said.

The portal appeared in front of him, and he stepped through it, disappearing from sight.

"You should go home as well," I told her, trying one last time. "We have this covered—especially now that we have the dragons on our side."

"Just because the mode of transportation has changed, it doesn't mean my plan to accompany you has changed," Hypatia said, joining us on board. "You'll still need me to create the portal back home for you once Typhon is defeated."

"We can fly them back to Kinsley in the chariot," the dragon leader offered. "With our speed, the trip should only take a few hours."

"That sounds like a good plan," I said to Hypatia. "We can spare those few hours, and that way you won't have to risk yourself."

"You *cannot* spare those few hours," she insisted. "What if something goes wrong? I hope it doesn't, but we need to plan for the worst. I'm coming with you, and that's the end of this discussion." She raised her chin in the air, signaling that the conversation was over, and I conceded.

If she insisted on coming, we couldn't stop her. And we didn't have the time to convince her otherwise. Plus, she had a good point. Hypatia had guided us correctly so far—I knew better than to question her decisions now.

"The equinox is close," the dragon leader warned us. "Typhon will rise soon. Prepare and brace yourselves, because we must fly to the mountain now."

He and the others shifted into their dragon forms. They stepped in front of the chariot, and fire flew out from it, connecting like reins to their bodies. Then they spread their wings, and I held onto the ledge of the chariot as they launched into flight, pulling us up with them and straight toward the rumbling mountain.

CHAPTER TWENTY-SEVEN

W e circled the sputtering mountain, waiting for the exact moment of the equinox. The dragons flew so smoothly that the floor of the chariot didn't even feel like it was moving beneath our feet. We stood strong and steady, staring out at the crater of the steaming volcano, ready for Typhon to rise.

Kate had Medusa's head out and ready. The gorgon's eyes were closed—it was too risky to keep them open—but Kate would open them the moment Typhon was looking at it.

"Which way will Typhon be facing when he rises from the crater?" I turned to Hypatia, figuring she was most likely to know the answer.

"There's no way to know," she replied. "But once he rises, we have to get around to the correct side as fast as possible—hopefully before he's aware that we're here." She glanced at her watch, the skin around her eyes creasing with worry. "One more minute until the equinox," she announced, and my heart raced, panic flooding my veins.

I reached for my bow, stringing an arrow through it and aiming it at the volcano. The others readied their weapons as well, even though physical weapons weren't their best method of defense—their elemental powers were.

Then the volcano exploded, booming so loudly that my head felt like it combusted right along with it. Smoke and ash rose from the crater, so thick that it blacked out my vision. My eyes burned, and I was forced to close them.

"I can't see!" I yelled, but the moment I breathed in, my lungs filled with ash and smoke. I coughed and sputtered, holding my hands in front of my mouth, unable to breathe. The others coughed as well.

At least the chariot was still flying, so the dragons must not be affected. Which made sense, since they were fire breathers.

I heard a loud, monstrous roar, so loud that the chariot vibrated from the strength of it—a sound that I dreaded came from Typhon himself. I tried to open my eyes again, but it was hopeless. All I saw was burning black ash before having to snap them shut. My eyes watered from the pain, tears rolling down my cheeks. I was holding my breath, trying to avoid breathing in the soot, but it was impossible. My lungs begged for air. My head pounded, dizzy from the lack of oxygen, and soon enough I was forced to give in and open my mouth for a breath.

When I did, the air was clear. I was still coughing, and each breath still hurt, but I could *breathe* again. I opened my eyes, rubbing away the soot so I could see. The ash around the chariot was gone—a bubble of clean air surrounded us. I couldn't see further since the area outside the bubble was pitch black with ash, as if we were inside looking out from inside a snow globe.

"What happened?" I tried to ask, but it came out as a croak, followed by another coughing fit. I called upon white energy, using it to heal myself from the smoke inhalation. Then I rested my hands on each of the others, healing them as well.

"What happened?" I asked again, speaking clearly this time.

"Ash and soot are part of the Earth," Kate explained. "I'm able to control it with my power. I'm going to have to clear it from around Typhon for us to be able to fight him. The moment I do, he'll know that we're here."

"We have no other choice," Blake said, standing strong and looking out in the direction of the volcano. "Do it."

She raised her arms, and the bubble pushed away the ash as it expanded, slowly revealing the gigantic monster. He was taller than a skyscraper, and he stood in the crater, his waist at its brim. Lava poured out of the volcano, traveling down the mountain and burning everything in its path.

I knew Typhon would be huge—larger than the monsters Scylla and Charybdis that we'd fought in Greece—but it still took all of my effort not to cower in fear, even though his back was toward us. He was covered in soot, but judging by his growls, he wasn't affected by it. Wings spanned from his shoulders—reminding me of the wings of a dragon—and snakes hissed and slithered around them. I shuddered as I realized that the snakes were *part* of him—they grew out of his scaly skin.

But I had no time to think, because the snakes shot fire at us—there must have been more than twenty of them in all. Blake raised his hands, blocking the flames. But he didn't just *block* the flames—he turned them around and boomeranged them back to where they came, burning away Typhon's wings.

Typhon roared, the sound nearly as loud as when the volcano erupted, throwing his hands down and arching his back in pain.

Danielle used the opportunity to gather water from the air and shoot it toward the snakes, drenching them and stopping them from shooting any more fire at us. They hissed and shot something else from their mouths —a thick, black gooey substance.

A glob of it landed on my arm, and I shrieked from the burning pain. I looked down and saw it burning its way through my skin. Poison. I ducked down so the walls of the chariot could shield me from more of the poison, and the others did the same.

Danielle must have seen the poison burning its way through my skin, because she aimed water toward it, washing away the black goo. Once it was gone, I healed my arm, letting out a long breath when the pain dissipated.

"Was anyone else hit?" I asked. Both Chris and Hypatia answered that they had been, and Danielle and I worked together to heal them as well.

But as we were working, the floor of the chariot started to tilt, and we slid toward the other side, balancing ourselves against its wall to keep ourselves from tumbling out over the edge.

Something must have happened to the dragons. They'd been immune to the flames... but they must not be immune to the poison. And they were too far away for me to reach out and heal them.

Perhaps their hides were strong enough to withstand it. But they shrieked from the pain, and then I heard a thud from below. It was followed by another thud, and then another.

I sneaked a peak over the edge of the chariot. Sure enough, only three dragons remained. The others had fallen into the lava, broken and motionless. Fire shot up around their charred bodies. Despite being creatures of fire, there was no way they could have survived that.

I averted my gaze and huddled back down, shaking at the sight of the death and devastation below. The remaining dragons had widened our circle, but the poison still shot around us. The snakes were stronger than I would have thought possible.

"We're coming around to the front of Typhon," Blake said, turning to Kate. "Use Medusa's head now!"

"I can't while the snakes are shooting their poison!" she said. "If the poison destroys her eyes before Typhon looks into them... she'll be useless."

"Then we have to kill the snakes." I got my bow ready and took a deep breath to prepare for the onslaught. Then I stood up, clearing my mind of all else but shooting the snakes in quick succession. They shot poison at me, but even though my body felt like it was on fire, I gritted through the pain. I just had to remind myself that each snake down was another step closer to defeating Typhon.

Danielle joined me, using her power to throw ice daggers at them. Chris also stood and used his power to throw knives at them, and Blake, Kate, and Hypatia shot them down with guns.

Typhon grunted as each snake died. He tried to swat at our chariot, but he was still stuck inside the crater of the volcano, and we remained out of his reach.

All the snakes were nearly gone. We were almost there. Just a few more...

But then another dragon went down. He hit the lava, and fire exploded around him. We only had two dragons left, and a quick glance over at them showed me that the poison was burning its way through their wings. They were flying slower... they weren't going to last much longer.

I shot more arrows—moving faster than humanly possible—letting them loose one after another until the final snake was dead. Once verifying that they were all gone, I ducked down again to huddle in the chariot, scrunching my eyes from the pain of the poison burning its way through my skin.

Danielle created a shower of rain above us to wash off the poison, the burning ceasing as it slid off my skin. Once it had all been washed away, I used my power to heal us.

Once finished, I glanced around at the others. Our clothes were wet and covered in soot, and we all looked like we had been to the Underworld and back, but we were alive. My energy level was lowering from having to use so much of it, but at least we were all okay. We just needed to get back around to the front of Typhon, and then we would use Medusa's head to do what we'd come here to do.

But the chariot jerked again, and when I looked ahead, only one dragon remained. He was flying more slowly than ever. It was the biggest dragon—the pack leader. Danielle had washed the poison off of him as well, but his hide was red and raw, his wings damaged and thin. Some parts were so thin that I could see straight through them. Every flap looked painful, as if his wings were about to rip apart.

I doubted he had much longer. And without a dragon left to fly the chariot, we would fall into the churning lava below. Despite our powers, I wasn't sure how we would survive that. We *needed* the dragon to live.

"Chris," I said, looking over at him. "Fly me out to the dragon so I can heal him."

"Good idea." He stood up and raised his hands in preparation to use his power. "Get ready."

Air billowed beneath my feet, lifting me up so I hovered over the floor of the chariot. I floated up higher, over the edge—and then I accidentally looked down at the hissing, flaming lava flow below. My stomach flipped at how high up I was, and I had to swallow down a wave of nausea. I couldn't even see any remnants of the fallen dragons. They must have been burned to ash and swallowed up by the lava.

"Keep flying!" I called out to the lone dragon, hoping the words of encouragement would help him to push on. "I'm coming over to heal you."

He twisted his head to look at me, his eyes dim with pain and defeat. But the movement must have been too much for him, because his wing split at its thinnest point, straight down the center, and his features contorted in pain.

"No!" I screamed, reaching forward to try to touch him. Only a few more feet. If he could hold on for a few seconds, I would be close enough to heal him.

But he let out a long breath, his eyes rolling back into his head, and tumbled down to the lava below.

CHAPTER TWENTY-EIGHT

I screamed, watching the dragon fall down and thump into the lava. Flames engulfed his body, and once they died out, all that remained was an unrecognizable lump where he'd landed. Then the lump disappeared, and the dragon was gone.

But even though the dragon had fallen, I remained floating where I was. I turned around and saw Chris standing on the chariot with his hands up in the air, his face scrunched in concentration. The chariot had dropped a few feet, but he seemed to be using his power to hold it—and me—steady. Everyone else on the chariot looked perfectly fine, and relieved to still be alive. Typhon still roared in the distance, trapped in the center of the crater, but for now, we were safe.

Chris flew me back to join them, and I took one

final glance down at where the dragon had fallen. I hadn't even known his name. Both times I'd made deals with him and his pack, I'd been too focused on getting what I wanted from him to complete our mission to bother to ask for their names.

And now, I would probably never find out.

I floated onto the floor of the chariot, and Blake rushed toward me, wrapping me in his arms. "Thank god you're safe," he said, pushing my hair off my face and studying me as if making sure I was really here. "When that dragon went down..." He shook his head, his eyes darkening. "I thought you would fall with him."

"I thought we *all* would fall." Danielle stood and attempted to brush the soot off her jeans, even though it was hopeless. "Chris—how long can you keep the chariot flying?"

"I'm not sure," he said, each word forced and strained. As he spoke, the chariot dropped a few inches.

"Don't waste your energy talking," I told him. "Bring us around to the front of Typhon so we can show him Medusa's head and end him once and for all."

I tried to sound confident, but truthfully, I was worried. Chris had lifted up the yacht on his own and flown it over Charybdis, but that was only because Zeus had given him the mint that had provided him with endless energy. The most he'd ever flown on his own was the five of us when we jumped from the tower of Chione's ice palace—and that flight had only lasted for a few seconds. Keeping the chariot afloat was using up more of his energy than I thought possible. How much longer would he be able to keep this up?

"We have to help him," I told the others. "Let's let him channel some of our energy too."

After healing the others and myself so many times, I was already getting depleted of my own energy, and I imagined that the others were running low as well. But we had to do everything we could do to help Chris. If that meant channeling him our energy until we were about to pass out, then so be it.

We all reached forward to touch Chris—everyone but Kate.

"Aren't you going to help?" Danielle asked her.

"I can't," Kate said, her voice sad. "I'm not mortal anymore. Now that I'm a goddess, the way that I access energy is different. Chris and I tried last week after we finished training. We thought that I could give him endless energy—like he had with Zeus's mint—but it didn't work. The fastest way to explain is that the energy that I access now is on a different wavelength— a wavelength you can't access. I can't access energy on your wavelength, either. But with the four of you helping him, it'll be enough. It *has* to be enough."

I nodded and focused on calling forth energy to channel it into Chris. From the ways the others were concentrating, I could tell they were doing the same. Our energy must have helped him, because the chariot flew around to face Typhon.

Typhon's head was ugly and enormous—larger than a house. He growled and raged, the ground shaking with his anger, the volcano flowing with more lava by the second and rumbling like it was about to burst. Luckily we were still far enough away that he couldn't reach us from where he was rooted in the center of the crater. But he wouldn't be stuck there forever. We needed to act fast.

"It's now or never." Kate stepped in front of us, raised Medusa's head high up in the air, and pried her eyes open.

Typhon's body wracked with an anguished howl, and then, he turned to stone.

CHAPTER TWENTY-NINE

The volcano was exploding with ash and lava one second, and quiet the next. Kate zipped Medusa's head back into the bag. None of us said anything—we just stared, speechless, at the giant stone statue of Typhon.

Then Chris stumbled, falling back onto the wall of the chariot. His skin was paler than I'd ever seen it. I couldn't imagine how heavy the chariot was—after all, it was made of all gold. Even with us channeling him what energy we had left, he still had to use his own to keep us afloat.

"Nicole," he said, looking at me. His voice was strained and weak, and he took a deep breath, forcing himself to continue. "Stop channeling your energy to me—you need as much of it as possible for what's next."

I knew what he meant—we'd discussed the plan multiple times back at Darius's house—so I knew he was right. Reluctantly, I broke my connection with Chris.

The chariot dropped, my stomach flipping at the sudden free fall, and I couldn't help it—I screamed.

But we only fell a few feet before Chris regained his hold.

He took another deep breath and flew the chariot toward the statue of Typhon towering up from the volcano, grunting from the effort. His clothes were soaked in sweat, and his eyes had gone bloodshot from the effort. The others still held onto him, although they looked pale and weak—they must not have much more energy to give him.

Which meant Chris was doing this mainly on his own.

Typhon was so huge that in our chariot, we were slightly smaller than the palm of his hand. We whizzed closer, and once we were in arm's reach, I placed both of my hands on the stone. Despite feeling weak from all the energy I'd used so far, I dug down deep to think about how much I *hated* this monster for the danger he was going to inflict on the world, and called forth the black energy. If he'd gotten his way, he was going to *destroy* the entire planet. The eruption had already destroyed the nearby villages in Sicily. And that only would have been the beginning. My friends, my family, our *lives*—all of it would have been gone. All because of this evil, heartless monster in front of me.

I gathered as much black energy as I could—until it felt like it was about to burst out of my skin—and shot it into the stone.

Cracks appeared all over. But Kate already held her arms out, her palms facing Typhon, using her power to keep him together so the stone didn't explode into pieces when we were right in front of it.

Chris flew us away, and I placed my hand on his arm again, giving him as much energy as I could. But after using so much black energy on Typhon, the energy I could collect and give to Chris was a mere trickle. I doubted it was doing much good, but I continued trying, since it was better than nothing.

Once there was enough distance between us and Typhon, Kate let go of her hold on the stone and the pieces shattered, hurtling into the lava and exploding into flames. The flames died down, the pieces of stone consumed by the molten rock below.

Then Kate raised her hands again and cooled the lava completely. It turned from orange to black, and the flames and hissing stopped. All that was below us now was thick, solid rock.

"The ground is safe," she told Chris. "You can lower us down now."

But as he lowered the chariot, he looked worse than ever. His breaths were shallow as he struggled to keep us afloat. He was hunched against the wall, using it as support, and his eyes were half shut and bloodshot. His hair stuck to his face, drenched with sweat. He didn't look like he could keep this up for much longer.

He got us more than halfway down, but when we only had a bit farther to go, the chariot tilted to the side. I screamed, gripping the ledge to keep myself from falling out.

Then he lost his hold on it completely and it tumbled to the ground.

CHAPTER THIRTY

My heart rose to my throat, and I screamed, my eyes meeting Blake's as we were thrown from the chariot. I landed feet first and tucked my chin to my chest to roll with the fall, relaxing my body and bending my knees just like Darius had taught us in training.

Each time I hit the ground, the air was knocked out of me. Finally I came to a stop. I rolled myself over and sucked in a deep breath, staring up at the ash-filled sky. I'd survived the fall. I'd been banged up, and my head was spinning, but as far as I could tell, I didn't have any serious injuries.

"Nicole!" someone screamed my name—Kate. "We need your help! Now!"

I moved my fingers, arms, ankles, and knees to see if

anything was broken. Everything seemed okay. Which was good, because I barely had any energy left—definitely not enough to fully heal myself. And I didn't know the extent of everyone else's injuries. I had to save my energy so I could heal one of them if they needed it.

I jumped up—my body ached at the sudden movement—and looked out to where Kate had called for me.

Chris was sprawled on the ground nearby, and Kate was hunched over him, sobbing. Blake was hobbling over to them—his ankle must have been injured, but other than that he seemed okay. Danielle had been thrown further to the side. She was just sitting up, and she cradled her wrist, which was twisted at an unnatural angle. The chariot was all the way off to the opposite side, upended so its wheels pointed out to the volcano.

I ran toward Kate, kneeling down next to her to look at Chris. His eyes were closed, and he was so pale and still.

Too still.

"He's not breathing," Kate sobbed. "I found him like this, and I don't know what happened to him when he fell, but he's not breathing. You have to heal him. Please. Heal him."

I nodded, and despite barely having enough energy

left to channel any more of it, I placed my hands on Chris to heal him.

I felt nothing.

It was just like when I'd tried to heal Rachael back in the hydra's cave, and when I'd tried to heal Kate after she'd been turned to stone, and when I'd tried to heal Blake after finding him slashed and mauled in a puddle of his blood in the cottage.

Chris's spirit was gone.

I pulled my hands away from him, tears falling from my eyes when I looked up at Kate. I blinked, not knowing what I could possibly say to her. So I just shook my head and lowered my eyes, hoping she understood.

"No." She pressed her lips together, refusing to believe me. "He didn't even get injured in the fall. Look at him! He looks fine. He must have…" She sat back on her heels and gasped, realization dawning in her eyes. "He wasn't strong enough to fly the chariot for that long, but he did it anyway, so we could kill Typhon," she said slowly. "He used up all his energy to save us. No… he used up all of his energy to save the *world*."

I nodded, not knowing what to say to her. I just felt… numb.

We'd succeeded in killing Typhon, but I still felt defeated. Chris had pushed his powers to the point of death so we could live. Without him, we would have fallen into that lava and died. It wasn't fair that he was gone.

But I knew enough about the pain Kate must be feeling right now—I'd felt the same way when I found Blake dead in that cottage—to know that nothing I said could help her. Instead, I placed my hand over hers, lowering my head and letting the tears fall.

"Nicole!" someone screamed my name and shook my shoulders—Danielle. She still cradled her wrist—from this close up, it was clearly broken—and her eyes were wide in panic.

I looked at her, preparing to tell her the news about Chris, but she continued before I could.

"Hypatia's stuck beneath the chariot," she said in a rush. "It must have landed on her when it fell. You have to come heal her—quick!"

CHAPTER THIRTY-ONE

I jolted back into focus and followed Danielle to the chariot. How had I missed this earlier? I'd seen the chariot when I'd landed, but I hadn't seen Hypatia near it.

As I approached, I realized why.

Hypatia was stuck around the opposite side, her lower half crushed under the golden vehicle. I couldn't see her injuries, but given the weight of the chariot, I assumed they were grave. She was pale—she must be losing blood—and her eyes were glassy and unfocused.

Blake hunched down next to her, holding her hand and comforting her. I imagined he'd been telling her that I was on my way.

But I barely had enough energy left after using so much of it during the fight with Typhon. I couldn't even heal my minor injuries. How was I supposed to heal someone who'd been crushed under a golden chariot?

I wasn't sure if I could, but I had to try.

"Nicole," Hypatia said my name, smiling when she saw me. Her voice was strained and weak—I could tell that speaking was painful for her. "I'm so glad you're here."

I kneeled down next to her, swallowing down fear as I placed my hand on her shoulder. "I'm glad I'm here, too." I tried to sound brave, even though I felt more helpless than ever. "I'm going to do everything I can to heal you. But first, we need to get this chariot off of you."

I looked up at the chariot, and doubt set into my mind. I couldn't imagine how heavy it would be. And with Blake's ankle injured, Danielle's wrist broken, and all three of us running low on energy, how were we supposed to pull this off?

But we stood up and braced ourselves against the chariot, ready to push. Blake counted to three, and we put all of our weight into it.

As suspected, it didn't budge. I grunted, pushing as hard as I could, but it still didn't move an inch. My head spun from the effort, spots dancing in front of my eyes, and I leaned against the chariot to catch my breath. I didn't have enough energy to push anymore.

Once I could see straight again, I stepped back and lowered my arms, looking helplessly at the chariot.

"We need Chris," Blake said. "Hopefully he has enough energy left over to help us out."

My heart dropped at the realization that Blake had been here with Hypatia the whole time. He still didn't know about Chris.

"Chris didn't make it." I dropped my hands to my sides, fresh tears forming in my eyes. "He used up all of his energy flying the chariot. He held on until the very end. When he lost control and we fell, it must have been because…" My throat thickened with tears, and I swallowed, unable to continue.

"Because he had no more energy left at all," Danielle finished my sentence.

Blake nodded and said nothing, apparently taking it all in. "He died a hero," he finally said. "We'll make sure that he's never forgotten. It's what he would want."

"It is." I sniffed, wiping the tears off my cheeks.

"We can't do anything for Chris anymore," Danielle reminded us softly. "We have to focus on who we *can* help—Hypatia. Chris wouldn't want us standing here crying over him when we could be saving her life."

I nodded and looked at the chariot again. There had to be another solution. Maybe we were approaching this from the wrong angle.

But as I walked around it, I saw that the land it was

on was completely flat. Once I came back around, I kneeled back down on the ground, no longer having enough energy to stand.

Pushing the chariot to the side would have been so much easier if it were on a hill.

I snapped my head up at the realization, hope surging through my chest. "Kate," I said her name, even though she was too far away to hear me. "If she can create a rift in the ground on the other side of the chariot, it'll be pulled down by its own weight. Gravity will take over. We won't have to push it."

Danielle's eyes lit up, and she hurried to fetch Kate before I could say another word. I was grateful for that, because I barely had enough energy to keep myself sitting up, let alone to run. In the meantime, I held Hypatia's hand, leaning against the chariot and trying my best to comfort her.

Danielle returned quickly with Kate. Kate looked shell-shocked by all that had just happened, but the moment she saw Hypatia trapped beneath the chariot, she snapped back into focus.

"I can fix this," she said to Hypatia. "You're going to be just fine."

Hypatia was too injured by now to speak—she must be losing blood fast—but she met Kate's eyes, her lips curving up into a small smile of thanks.

Kate held out her hands, and the ground rumbled, a

crack forming on the opposite side of the chariot. It teetered on the ledge, and Blake gave it another push.

As predicted, gravity took over and it fell in, revealing the horrible remains of Hypatia's lower body.

Her legs were crushed, but that wasn't the worst of it. The chariot had gashed her abdomen, and now that the chariot wasn't holding everything together, her intestines were slowly making their way out of her stomach. I gasped, reaching for them to push them back in, but I had no idea where they were supposed to go. Blood covered my hands—blood was everywhere. It was coming out too quickly to stop it.

Spots danced in front of my eyes again, but I took a deep breath, forcing myself to focus. "I'm going to need your help," I told Blake and Danielle. "I used up too much energy in the fight with Typhon. I don't think... I *know* I don't have enough left to heal her."

"I used most of mine in the fight and when we were channeling it to Chris," Blake said. "But I'll help as much as I can."

"Me too," Danielle said, and both of them put their hands on my arms, ready to channel what they could of their remaining energy.

With both hands pressed against Hypatia's stomach, I reached out to the Universe, trying to feel the white energy around me. It was faint—barely within reach. But somehow, I pulled some of it toward me. A tiny bit, and then a tiny more. It was a trickle entering my body —but it was better than nothing.

"What's happening?" Danielle asked, her voice worried. "Shouldn't it be working by now?"

I said nothing, not wanting to break my concentration. If I did, I worried that I would lose the small amount of white energy that I *had* managed to collect.

But the trickle was getting less and less, and given Hypatia's injuries, we were running out of time. I had to use what I had gathered so far and hope for the best.

I sent the small amount of white energy that I'd collected into her body, although I knew before opening my eyes that it wouldn't be enough. The amount I'd been able to collect had only been enough to heal a few scratches. The gash in her stomach hadn't healed—it looked the exact same as it had before I'd tried to heal her. Her intestines were only staying in place because I was holding them there. And the pool of blood around her body was growing. It had traveled so far that by now, I was kneeling in it.

"It's not working," I said, my voice cracking. "We have to get to the hospital. Hypatia—do you have enough energy left to create a portal?"

She opened her mouth to speak, but then her eyes glazed over, and she was gone.

CHAPTER THIRTY-TWO

I used my pendant to call to Apollo for help. He didn't come for us, but he stopped by Darius's and told Jason to create a portal for us to come home. I barely remember walking through the portal—I was in so much shock—but we did bring Chris and Hypatia's bodies with us.

The next few days passed in a blur. My family tried to cheer me up over Easter, but the time spent with them didn't feel real. It was like I was separated from my body, looking down on everything as I pretended to act as normal as I could manage. All I could think about was Chris's upcoming funeral. The only small comfort I had was that after his great sacrifice, he would almost surely be sent to Elysium—the Greek equivalent to Heaven.

On the night of the funeral, Blake, Danielle, Kate, and I returned to Chris's gravestone. He'd been buried next to the statue of Zeus, which was appropriate, given that Zeus was his godly ancestor. The cemetery had been packed that afternoon during the service, but now, it was only the four of us.

We brought the Book of Shadows with us, because despite defeating Typhon, our mission wasn't over. There was one last thing for us to do. But to get started on that task, we needed to ask the Book of Shadows an important question. We wanted Chris to be with us for that, and this—asking at his burial spot—was the closest we would get to that happening.

Kate brought out the Book of Shadows, placed it on top of Chris's gravestone, and rested her hands on the cover. "Ready?" she asked, looking around at each of us.

We all nodded in response.

"How do we seal the portal to Kerberos?" she asked, her voice echoing through the cemetery.

The book glowed, and she gasped, yanking her hands off the cover. It opened on its own, the pages flipping themselves, as if they were being controlled by the wind—or as if possessed by a spirit. The glow illuminated our faces, and we stared at the Book, waiting for whatever it wanted to show us.

But the Book didn't select a page. Instead, it slammed itself shut.

The air behind it glimmered, and standing before us was Nyx herself.

CHAPTER THIRTY-THREE

Nyx wore the same black gown that she'd had on the first time we met her—the billowing skirt full of sparkling stars that twinkled with her every movement. Her skin was as pale as moonlight, her hair dark as night.

"I received your question," she said, glancing at the Book. "I have much to tell you, and I thought that answering through the pages would be far from satisfactory. So, I decided to pay you a visit myself."

"*You've* been the one answering our questions through the Book this entire time?" Kate asked.

"Yes," Nyx answered. "As you know, thousands of years ago I filled a comet with my magic and sent it across the sky, creating the portal to Kerberos and giving the Olympian gods the strength to lock the

Titans inside. But portals between worlds need more than the magic of the gods to keep them closed. They also need the magic of mortals who can bind them to the planet—in this case, to Earth. And so, I chose five mortals for this task and arranged that they all ended up in this town."

"You mean us," Kate breathed.

"Yes," Nyx said. "I chose the group of you."

"But they all grew up here," I chimed in. "I didn't. I grew up in Georgia."

"This is true." Nyx nodded. "There was no need for me to arrange for your arrival until your powers were unblocked. You see, some of the Head Elders see demigods as dangerous, and centuries ago, they created a spell to block demigods from using their powers. But a few months ago, I filled the comet with magic again. This time the magic would connect the five chosen mortals—the five of you—to the elements. The magic in that comet also unblocked the powers of demigods all over the world."

"Why did you choose us?" Danielle asked, looking around at our group. "We're all so… different."

"Each member of a team should have different strengths, and the five of you have that," Nyx said. "Your personalities embody the characteristics of your element, and your dominant heritages—the godly ancestor whose bloodline is strongest in you—give you even better control over those elements. Aphrodite was born from the sea, Ares has a fiery temperament, Zeus has power over the sky, Athena is level headed and down to earth, and Apollo has an affinity for healing. Their blood in your veins reinforced your connection to your element.

"But due to your differences, you would not have worked together unless you had a push from the gods. So I designed your first mission—the 'scavenger hunt' around town, as you called it—to teach you how to use your powers, work together, and trust one another."

"You designed that whole thing?" I asked. "Even the prophecy that we were given in the beginning?"

"Yes." Nyx nodded. "The mission needed to have a starting point. So I visited a young witch in her dreams a few centuries ago and gave her the prophecy that would ultimately land into your hands and begin your journey."

"What about the harpy?" Blake asked. "You planned on her being there, too? And on her kidnapping Nicole's sister?"

"No," Nyx answered. "I placed the Book of Shadows near the portal to Kerberos so that you could learn the location of the portal. You were supposed to grab the Book, bring it back to Darius's house, and then use it to ask me questions. The harpy acted on her own free will—although I do feel as though her being there pushed you to train faster and harder."

"We almost died fighting her," Danielle said.

"But you didn't." Nyx smiled. "And if you had… I could have convinced Chronos to allow me to travel through time and correct that mistake."

I shivered, wondering how many timelines the primordial deities had created and destroyed. I had a feeling that I didn't want to know. Especially because technically, this was the only timeline that actually existed. All the other ones were gone.

"We're getting off track," Kate said. "I mean, this is all very interesting, and I'll have lots of questions later, but our original question still hasn't been answered. How do we seal the portal to Kerberos?"

"I suppose it's time that you learned," Nyx said with a sigh. "Although I fear that you're not going to like the answer."

"It doesn't matter if we like the answer or not," Blake said. "We need to know it if you want us to have any chance of closing the portal."

"I know," Nyx said. "I just wanted you to be prepared. You remember what I said earlier, about how the magic of mortals is the only thing that can seal the portal forever?"

"Yes," I said, anxious for her to continue.

"That's because the portal is in between the worlds

of Kerberos and Earth," she said. "The worlds are pushing against each other, which has worn down the portal over time and weakened it. It will open fully on the summer solstice, unless you use your powers to close it permanently. To do that, you need to bind both sides of the portal with physical elemental magic from Earth, and then seal it with the power of spirit."

"Okay," I said, although I was still confused. "How exactly do we do that?"

"This is the part you're not going to like," she said. "The final part is the easy part—once the portal is strengthened by the binding, Nicole will have to touch it and fill it with spirit to seal it and make the binding permanent. But it's the binding that's more complex." She paused, her eyes dimming, and she rested a hand on top of Chris's gravestone. She looked more vulnerable than I'd imagined possible for a primordial deity.

I could barely breathe as I stared at her, waiting for her to go on. The others were silent as well.

"To bind the portal, one mortal with physical elemental magic has to be on the Earth side of the portal, and the other has to be on the Kerberos side," she continued. "Together, they will press their palms over their side of the portal and fill it with their Earthly elemental magic. This will temporarily bind the portal, returning it to full strength so Nicole can seal it to keep it that way."

"Okay." Blake nodded. "So one of us has to enter Kerberos again. Since Kate is a goddess and can't pass through the portal, it'll have to be either me or Danielle. Then, once we finish binding it, we'll return to Earth."

"It won't be that easy," Nyx said sadly. "Because once the portal is bound, it'll be strengthened again. Passing back through will be impossible."

CHAPTER THIRTY-FOUR

Whoever went to the other side of the portal would never be able to return.

The realization hit me like a ton of bricks, and my mind raced, desperate for another solution.

"Why do we have to bind the portal at all?" I asked. "Why can't I seal it with my magic as it is right now?"

"You cannot." Nyx shook her head. "You went against my instructions and tried that in another timeline. We learned that if you seal the portal before the binding, you'll seal it in the weakened condition that it's in right now. Which means monsters will still be able to cross through it at will. In that timeline, the Titans eventually crafted a way to blast through the weakened portal and take over the Earth. Once that happened,

Chronos allowed me to pass through a time portal to try again."

"So you're saying that one of us has to volunteer to bind the portal from the Kerberos side, and that person will end up stuck there forever," Danielle clarified. "Correct?"

"Yes," Nyx answered. "I wish there were another way, but unfortunately, no war is ever won without sacrifice. There's no other option."

"We don't know that," I said. "There's still time to figure out something else. We have *months* until the summer solstice."

"Three months," Kate jumped in.

"And the longer you wait, the more monsters will escape through the portal," Nyx said. "It's best to seal it sooner rather than later."

"I know that." I clenched my fists, determined not to give in that easily. "But what if we can research and figure out another way to close the portal? A way that doesn't involve one of us getting stuck in Kerberos forever?" I swallowed back tears, desperate to find a solution. Because like Blake had said, the person in Kerberos would have to be either him or Danielle.

I had a dreadful feeling that Blake would try to be brave and volunteer.

I couldn't let that happen. I'd just gotten him back. I couldn't lose him again.

"You said the same thing before," Nyx said. "You found nothing—this is the only time a portal to another world has been opened from Earth, so there was no information on the subject. But you decided to try sealing the portal without binding it anyway. Like I said, it did not work."

"If this is the only time a portal has been opened to another world from Earth, then how do you know this is the only way we can seal it?" I asked.

"I'm a primordial deity," Nyx reminded us—as if we needed reminding. "Which means I don't just rule over Earth—I rule over *all* the planets in the Universe. Portals to other worlds *have* been opened on other planets before. Binding the portal with the elements from one of the planets and then sealing it with spirit is the only way to close it. I wish I had another answer for you, but I don't. I'm sorry."

"I thought we couldn't even access our powers from Kerberos," Danielle said. "If we can't access our powers, how are we supposed to use them to bind the portal?"

"As long as you're touching the portal, you'll be able to use your powers," Nyx answered. "But the moment the portal is sealed, that connection will be severed."

"You *knew* the portal couldn't be sealed without our help," I said, unable to keep the anger from my tone. "So why did you create it at all?"

"The Titans had already escaped Tartarus—the one

place in the underworld of Earth that's supposed to be inescapable," Nyx said. "During the Second Rebellion, I saw two possible futures for Earth—a bright one full of the greatest technological innovation I've ever witnessed, or a dark one full of chaos and destruction. The former was what would happen if the Olympians won, and the latter was what would happen if the Titans won. I *wanted* the Olympians to win, so I interfered, creating the portal to Kerberos and helping them lock the Titans inside. Then I closed the portal, but I knew it wouldn't last forever—that permanently sealing it would have to wait until it weakened enough for mortals to pass through. Now, it's your responsibility to complete what I started all of those thousands of years ago—to ensure that the Titans remain in Kerberos forever."

"Okay." Danielle nodded. If she was scared, she didn't show it. "I suppose, on one level, I can understand that. But why did you wait until now to tell us? Why not tell us earlier, so we had more time to research other options, or to prepare?"

"Telling you earlier wouldn't have changed the inevitable," Nyx said. "There was no point in worrying about who would bind the portal without knowing which of you would survive to this point. Plus, knowing earlier only would have made everything harder for you. It would have distracted you from your previous missions."

"Let me guess how you know this," I said, past caring about being snarky to a goddess. She might have put us in this position, but it didn't mean we had to be happy about it. "You told us earlier in another timeline? And it didn't work out?"

"Yes." Nyx nodded. "In that timeline, you all became distracted and reckless. By this point, you were all dead, so the portal could not be closed."

"If we keep failing, why do you always choose to give *us* powers over the elements?" Kate asked. "Why not choose some other mortals—ones who won't give you this much trouble?"

"As I explained earlier, the five of you are uniquely suited to controlling your elements," Nyx said. "Witches are rare enough—let alone witches with your precise bloodlines and temperaments. There is no one else to choose." She paused to look at each of us, her eyes dark and serious. "I know this is a lot for you to process. But remember—the world is counting on you to make the right decision. This responsibility is yours, and yours alone."

Then she swished her dress around herself, and she was gone.

CHAPTER THIRTY-FIVE

Nyx wasn't all that had disappeared—the Book of Shadows was gone as well. Now that she'd given us our final task, apparently she didn't think we needed it as a direct line to ask her questions anymore.

I swallowed, not knowing what to do. Sacrificing either Blake or Danielle to Kerberos couldn't be the only way to keep the Titans from destroying the Earth. Or at least, that's what I *wanted* to believe.

But I had a sinking feeling that Nyx was telling us the truth.

"I wish it could be me," Kate broke the silence, resting her hand on the top of Chris's gravestone. "After all, I'm not even supposed to be here. I was supposed to have died back when we fought Medusa."

"No." I gasped, shocked that it had even crossed her

mind. "You're supposed to be right here, where you are now. I have no idea what the future has in store for you, but whatever it is, you'll do great things. I know it."

"Thanks." She smiled, although it didn't reach her eyes. "But if I could walk through that portal, I would volunteer in a heartbeat."

I knew she meant it. But I supposed that level of self-sacrifice was what made Kate qualified to successfully complete the apotheosis, while most others were not. Whatever she chose to stand for as a goddess, she would be giving to the good of the Earth long past when the rest of us were gone. She was going to do great things with her immortal life. She belonged here —not in Kerberos.

None of us belonged in Kerberos. But either Blake or Danielle would be stuck there anyway. It wasn't fair. Why did we have to go through so much, only to be forced into an impossible decision like this one?

"I wish Chris were here," Kate spoke again, looking sadly at his gravestone. "He would crack *some* kind of joke that would make this situation feel not as dark and daunting."

"He might try," I said. "But I don't think even Chris could make this feel any less difficult than it is."

"I miss him," Kate said, wrapping her arms around herself. "We spent a lot of time together in the past week... but I never got to tell him how I felt about him.

I was going to wait until this was all over. But now he'll never know."

"He knew," Danielle said, as confident as ever. "And he felt the same way about you."

"Maybe." Kate shrugged. "But it couldn't have worked out between us, anyway. After all, I'm immortal now. He wasn't. I was going to have to watch him die sooner or later." She gazed out at the statue of Zeus, her eyes distant.

"I just wish it hadn't been so soon," I said.

"Me either," she said, snapping back into focus. "But none of that matters, because he's gone, and he's never coming back. All we can do now is move forward."

"You're right," Blake agreed, stepping forward. "We need to close that portal as soon as possible. And we won't have to worry about the big decision, because I've already made it. I'm going to be the one to bind the portal from Kerberos."

CHAPTER THIRTY-SIX

"No." I grabbed onto his hand, as if that would be enough to make him stay. "I just got you back. If you do this... you'll be gone. Forever. I'll never be able to see you again." I stared up at him and blinked away tears, begging him to take it back.

But I knew deep in my heart that he wouldn't.

"There are only two options for who can close the portal from Kerberos," Danielle reminded me. "Me or Blake. Are you saying that you want *me* to be the one to do it?"

"No," I stuttered, since it was the truth. "I don't want *either* of you to do it."

"That's not an option," she said. "One of us has to do it. And... I wouldn't blame you if you wanted it to be me."

I didn't reply this time, because as much as I wanted to tell her she was wrong, I couldn't. Yes, Danielle and I had learned to work together, and we didn't completely hate each other anymore, but I *loved* Blake. If one of them had to sacrifice themselves, I didn't want it to be him.

But he'd already offered himself. And I didn't expect Danielle to volunteer anytime soon.

We had to figure out something else.

"If you're closing the portal from the Kerberos side, then I'm going with you," I told Blake. "Nyx said I have to use Spirit to seal the portal—but she didn't say which side of the portal I had to be on to do that. So I'll do it from the Kerberos side. I won't let you get stuck there alone."

"Think about what you're saying." Blake took both of my hands in his, his eyes sad and resolved. "Sealing the portal will stop the war, but all of those creatures who escaped between the time the portal first opened and the time we closed it will still be out there. Not to mention the fact that all of the demigods who recently had their powers awakened—who knows how many of them there are—will need to learn about who they are and what they can do. You can help them. The world needs you *here*, Nicole. Not in Kerberos. You can't sacrifice yourself unnecessarily."

"Maybe you're right," I told him. "But I need *you*

here. So if I need you here and the world needs me here, then that means you have to stay here, too."

"You don't need me." He smiled sadly, tracing his thumb over my cheekbone. "You might *want* me here with you, but you're strong. You'll be able to move on without me. You'll have to."

"You're wrong." I shook my head, and unable to stop the tears anymore, the floodgates opened. "I can't let you do this. Not after I just lost you and got you back. We've been through so much together—I can't imagine my future without you in it."

"You'll have to," he said. "Because if I don't do this, then there won't be any future for the world at all. And what about your family? Your mom, your step-dad, your sister, and even Apollo. Do you really want to leave them when you don't have to?"

"You have a family, too," I told him. "I'm sure you don't want to leave them either."

"I don't have a choice," he said. "You do."

I glanced at Danielle, wishing she would step up and volunteer herself. Shouldn't she feel guilty that Blake volunteered and she was letting him walk into that hell world without even contemplating sacrificing herself? The two of them had dated for months. Their relationship had fallen apart, but she'd cared for him at one point. That had to mean something.

But she refused to meet my eyes, and she said nothing.

Even if there was a part of her that still cared about Blake, there was one person she cared about more—herself. After all these past few weeks of fighting to save the world, I thought she would have changed. Clearly I was wrong. She was just as selfish as ever.

"There has to be another option," Kate said, finally breaking the silence.

"There's not." I couldn't keep the anger from my tone. "Nyx said there wasn't. The only other option is for Danielle to volunteer, but she's too selfish to do that when Blake's already volunteered to take the fall for her."

"That's not fair." Danielle jutted her chin out. "We have *weeks* until the portal opens. You can't ask me to volunteer when I've barely had time to think this through."

"Every day that the portal remains weakened, more monsters can come through," I reminded her.

"We can fight them," she insisted. "I would rather do that than volunteer to trap myself in a hell dimension for all of eternity without taking time to think about it."

"Blake volunteered," I said. "He volunteered the *moment* he heard it was the only way to save the world."

"And you volunteered to follow him right in there."

She sneered. "Sorry that we can't all be as noble. Or as impulsive."

"Stop it!" Kate rubbed her temples, as if listening to us was giving her a headache. "Fighting isn't going to get us anywhere. But there has to be another option—one that doesn't involve sacrificing another one of us. What we need to do is *think*."

"About what?" I asked. "Nyx already told us that there's no other option. We've searched and tried in other timelines. We were never able to come up with anything. Why would that change now?"

"Then we need to outthink ourselves," Kate said. "Where's the first place we would go to look for answers?"

"The New Alexandrian Library," Danielle answered quickly. "Easy."

"Then we have to assume that we've already checked there in another timeline," Kate said. "So where else can we look?"

"We could ask the Head Elders from each territory," Blake suggested. "Maybe they would have other ideas about where to look for answers."

"Good idea." Kate nodded. "Now let's assume that in another timeline, we've tried that as well. Where should we look next?"

"Olympus," I piped in, instinctively grabbing my sun

pendant. "The Olympians might have ideas that we wouldn't think of ourselves."

"They might," Kate said. "But in another timeline, we probably came to the same conclusion."

"And the primordial deities would know more than the Olympians," Danielle added. "Since they're more powerful."

I narrowed my eyes at her, taking a deep breath to calm myself and stop myself from trying to strangle her. How had I managed to get along with her for the past few weeks? She was just as awful as she'd been when I first moved to Kinsley. I'd just been so focused on completing our mission that I'd been blinded to what a horrible, selfish person she was.

At least I now knew better than to let that happen again.

We threw out another round of ideas, but again, Kate kept saying that we'd likely tried them already. We needed to think outside of the box. She made it sound so easy, but who knew more than the primordial deities themselves?

That was when it came to me.

"The Oracle." I looked at each of them, knowing this idea was better than any we'd had yet. "The gods might not be able to see the exact future, but the Oracle can."

CHAPTER THIRTY-SEVEN

"The Oracle *would* have an answer for us." Kate chewed on her lower lip. "But the Oracle's dead. She's been dead for thousands of years."

"But she's in the Underworld," Danielle added. "She wasn't locked in Kerberos."

"True." Kate stared at Danielle, her eyes wide. "But we can't just march into the Underworld and chat with her. In all of history, only a handful of people have journeyed there and back."

"Why not add one more person to that list?" I asked. "After everything we've been through, I don't see why marching into the Underworld to chat with the Oracle is that far fetched of an idea."

"Are you volunteering?" Danielle asked. "Because you know that if you go down to the Underworld, there's no knowing if you'll be allowed back up to Earth. And without you here, it'll be impossible to seal the portal."

"Even more of a reason why it should be me that goes," I said. "We've heard from both Nyx *and* Erebus that if the Titans come back to Earth, they'll destroy everything in this dimension—including the Underworld. Which means that Hades, the king of the Underworld, wants the portal sealed just as much as the gods up on Olympus. He'll have no choice but to let me back up to Earth."

"Not just you." Blake stepped up to my side. "You're not going down there alone. I'm going with you."

"You already volunteered to bind the portal from Kerberos." I could barely get the words out, hating that they were the truth. "You can't risk yourself by going to the Underworld, too."

"Yes, I can," he said. "They need me back on Earth if they want that portal closed, too. If you're going, I'm going. No questions about it."

"There's one big flaw in your logic," Kate said, holding a hand up. "What if the Oracle *does* know about another way to close the portal? And what if that way doesn't involve both of you needing to be there?"

I bit my lower lip, unable to come up with an answer. Because as always, Kate had a good point.

It looked like we were back to square one.

But then the ground swirled nearby, until the dust was as tall as a person, clearing to reveal a beautiful woman. She wore a long green dress, and flowers were woven through her long red hair. I'd never met her before, but due to her dramatic entrance and divine appearance, I figured it was safe to assume that she was a goddess.

"You won't need to worry about not being allowed back to Earth, because I will accompany you to the Underworld and make sure you're returned here safely," she said, her lips turning up in a small smile. "And Hades certainly won't refuse *my* request... because I am his wife, the Queen of the Underworld."

CHAPTER THIRTY-EIGHT

"Persephone?" Kate blinked, staring up at the goddess.

"Yes." The goddess smiled, seemingly pleased that Kate was able to identify her so quickly. "You must be Kate. The transition to being a goddess suits you nicely. Once our business with ending the war with the Titans is finished, I do hope that we'll become friends."

Kate opened her mouth, closed it, and then nodded in return. Apparently, being acknowledged by a goddess as an equal had left her speechless.

"How did you know we needed help?" Danielle asked Persephone, getting straight to business. "In the past, it's only been the primordial deities who've come to us spontaneously. We've always needed to call for the Olympians when we wanted to speak with them."

"It's true that we are not omniscient," Persephone said. "We cannot be everywhere at once. However, since your return to Kinsley, the messenger god Hermes has been keeping an eye on you. He came to fetch me the moment you started discussing journeying to the Underworld, and he told me of your plan. I spend half the year in the Underworld and the other half on Earth, and I just returned for my time on Earth. I treasure my time on Earth, but I think your plan is a good one, so I'm here to help."

"You'll take me and Nicole to the Underworld to speak with the Oracle?" Blake asked.

"Don't forget me and Kate," Danielle added. "If this is happening, we're going, too." She turned to Kate, her brow raised in question. "Right?"

Kate wrung her hands together, looking deep in thought. "As much as I would be curious to visit the Underworld and speak with the Oracle, I don't think us joining would be the best use of our time," she said. "Remember—we only have a few weeks to figure out a solution. It makes the most sense to split up into pairs to try to figure out an alternative way to seal the portal. While Blake and Nicole are in the Underworld, we should be researching other options."

"Very wise." Persephone nodded. "Spoken like a true descendant of Athena." She smiled at Kate, and then turned to me and Blake. "I also cannot promise that

Hades will allow you to speak with the Oracle. I can support your request, and I expect him to fully consider it, but it's not guaranteed. I will, however, do everything in my power to urge him to listen."

"Thank you," I told her. "We appreciate your help very much."

And if Hades doesn't listen to your request, then we'll just have to go against his wishes and find the Oracle ourselves.

Although, of course I didn't say that last part out loud. We would deal with that if it came to it. But I didn't think it would—because from the fire in Persephone's eyes when she looked at me and Blake, I guessed that she would do everything in her power to provide us an audience with the Oracle.

"So... how do we get to the Underworld?" I asked her. "Can you portal us there?"

"Portals cannot be created to or within the Underworld," she answered. "If the souls there could create portals out of their assigned realms, it would be utter chaos. Instead, we must portal to the in-between, and the ferryman will transport us to the gates."

She raised her hands in the air, and then, right next to Chris's grave, a swirling portal appeared.

CHAPTER THIRTY-NINE

T he portal was dark blue, like the ocean, and I couldn't see through it.

What if Persephone was sending us to the Underworld and didn't intend on coming with us? What if she refused to bring us back home? I wanted to trust her... but recently I'd learned not to blindly trust *anyone*, even if they seemed like they were on your side.

Before jumping, I had to make sure this wasn't a trap.

"You'll definitely bring us back to Kinsley when we're ready to come home?" I asked Persephone. "You swear it upon Zeus?"

"Yes." The goddess nodded. "I swear upon Zeus that I will bring you and Blake back to Kinsley when you're ready. I will even step through the portal to the in-between first, to show you that I don't intend to abandon you."

Without waiting for our response, she stepped through the portal, disappearing from view. Blake and I looked at each other, and he grabbed my hand.

I looked down at our intertwined fingers, sadness filling my heart. How much longer would he be here with me? Had I fallen in love with him only to lose him forever, after not nearly enough time spent together?

But I straightened, forcing the dark thoughts from my mind. We were going on this mission to find another way to save the world. A way that wouldn't involve Blake having to sacrifice himself.

"Ready?" he asked me, his eyes intense and serious.

"Ready," I answered, and together, we stepped through the portal.

CHAPTER FORTY

The ground disappeared beneath my feet, and I was falling down a dark hole. My stomach rose into my throat, and I screamed, falling farther and farther with no signs of stopping.

I'd never gone skydiving before, but I imagined this was what it was like. Except while skydiving, you could see what was around you. And you had a parachute. We were just freefalling down to the in-between, blind, with no idea when we would stop.

I held tightly onto Blake's hand as I fell. In those terrifying moments, he was all that existed to me in this empty, dark world. If he ended up stuck in Kerberos, what would I do without him? Tears escaped my eyes at the thought, but I was falling so quickly that they dried right off my cheeks, as if they'd never existed at all.

Then, when it felt like we'd been falling forever and would never stop, my feet landed softly on the ground.

I looked around to get my bearings. I was standing at the bank of an underground river. Fog rose from the water, dampness filling the air. A canoe was banked on the ledge closest to us, and a man in a hooded cape stood at the back of it, holding a single oar. The cape hid the majority of his body—all I could see of him was a pair of glowing red eyes.

Persephone stood in front of him, looking out of place in the dark cave. "Hello, Charon," she greeted the hooded man, pulling three golden coins out of a pocket in her dress and handing them to him. "One coin for each of us, as per your usual fare."

"That *is* my usual fare," he said, his voice low and craggily. "However, those two mortals do not belong in the Underworld." He pointed to me and Blake and jammed his oar into the ground. "They are still alive. I only transport the souls of those who have passed on. You, my Queen, should be well aware of the rules."

Persephone reached back into her pocket and pulled out two more coins. "Will you transport them for twice the normal fare?" she asked.

He eyed the coins, his eyes glowing brighter. "I do not break the rules for simply anyone," he said, his focus still on the money. "However, for five times the normal fare, I will agree to it this once."

"You drive a hard bargain." Persephone kept her gaze level with his. "But I am your Queen, and I do not appreciate being taken advantage of. Three times the regular fare seems like an agreeable compromise, does it not?"

"Fine." He grunted. "But pay up now, before I change my mind."

She handed him the extra coins, and he counted them, taking his time to make sure each one was there. Once finished, he moved his oar aside so we could step on board. His movements were slow, like an old man. How could he have the strength to row us down the river? But Persephone trusted him, and I trusted that she wouldn't lead us astray.

She motioned for us to board first, and Blake held out his hand to assist me stepping onto the canoe. I instinctively reached to take it, but then I pulled back. Because soon, there was a chance that Blake wouldn't be here for me any longer. And even though stepping onto the canoe was a small thing, I needed to prove to myself that I didn't need his help. That I would be fine without him.

But as I stepped on board and settled into the seat, I knew I was lying to myself. I wouldn't be fine without him. I might be able to convince everyone else that I was moving on, but I would always wonder what could have been if he hadn't sacrificed himself.

Why had he been so quick to offer himself to bind the portal from Kerberos? It wasn't fair of me to be angry at him for it, but I couldn't help myself. I couldn't even look at him as the canoe started to make its way down the river. The fact that he'd sacrificed himself so quickly *hurt*. Why was he so willing to leave me? Did he not love me as much as I loved him?

I curled my legs up to my chest and wrapped my arms around them, looking out at the foggy river as we rowed along. I knew I was being silly—of course Blake loved me—but it was impossible to stop the doubt from creeping into my mind. His offering to sacrifice himself felt like he'd ripped out a piece of my heart. And I didn't know if it would be possible to repair. Because even if we found another way and he didn't have to sacrifice himself, he'd *offered* after barely taking any time to think about it. He was okay with the idea of leaving me. And he didn't want me to go with him. That hurt more than I could ever possibly say.

He scooted closer to me, his shoulder touching mine. "Are you cold?" he asked, running his hands along my arm. "You have goose bumps."

"I'm fine." I pulled my arm away from him, his touch only making my heart hurt more.

His eyes darkened—I could tell that I was hurting him—but I didn't know what else to do or say to him right now.

So I did the first thing that crossed my mind—I changed the subject. "Where are we now?" I asked Persephone, turning around to look at her. "How much longer until we reach the Underworld?"

"We're traveling along the Acheron River," Persephone replied. "Charon transports the souls of the dead along the river until reaching the Gates of the Underworld."

"So that's where we're heading to now," I said. "To the gates."

"Yes." She nodded. "It should only take about an hour to arrive."

A soft wailing filled the area, and I looked around, trying to see where it was coming from. There was nothing there. Except for the fog, of course. But then I heard it again, and I knew I couldn't be imagining it.

"What was that?" I asked, the goose bumps on my arms rising further. "You all heard that, right? That... crying sound. Like someone's hurt."

Another cry—this one a scream—filled the air. I turned to Persephone, since surely she must have heard it that time, and waited for an answer.

"The Acheron is also known as the River of Pain." She was as calm as ever as she explained, as if she were a teacher taking us on a field trip. "The river is the embodiment of all the suffering throughout the Earth, and the cries of those in pain echo across its waters. But do not be alarmed, as the river will not bring *you* any pain. It washes away the pain of all those who immerse themselves within its waters. But please, don't jump in yourselves. Many who do become so content with the numbness that they remain in limbo, stuck in its depths forever."

I scooted to the edge of the boat and looked down into the water. It was covered in fog, so thick that I could barely see the surface. What I could see of the surface was dark—the water in this river must run deep.

Did the river only heal physical pain? Or did it heal emotional pain, too? I rested my arm on the ledge of the boat, tempted to dip my fingers in and see what happened. If the waters of the Acheron could help me feel like my heart wasn't about to break into pieces, I needed to know.

The fog danced around my hand, and I lowered my arm further, ready to dip my fingers into the water and find out for myself.

CHAPTER FORTY-ONE

"**W**hat are you doing?" Blake wrapped his hand around my wrist and pulled my arm back into the boat, his eyes flashing with concern. "Didn't you hear Persephone? That water is dangerous."

"Only if we jump in." I yanked my hand out of his grip and dropped it into my lap. "I was just going to touch it. Nothing would have happened."

"You can't just go dipping your fingers into the Rivers of the Underworld." He clenched his fists and took a few breaths to calm himself. "Promise me you won't try anything like that again, okay?" he asked. "If anything happened to you..." He shook his head, his eyes pained at the thought. "I won't be able to live with myself if anything bad happens to you while we're here."

I turned away from him, refusing to make him that promise. Why should I? *He* was the one offering to sacrifice himself to Kerberos. And he had the nerve to tell me that he wouldn't be able to live with himself if anything bad happened to *me.*

It made no sense.

Because why did he think that I would be any less affected by his loss than he would be by mine?

WE SPENT the rest of the ride down the river in silence. As I looked around, listening to the cries and screams echoing across the water, all I could think about was Blake ending up in Kerberos, and the pain and grief that he would suffer while there. No one aged in Kerberos, so he would be trapped there for eternity. And if he *did* die while there, he would go to the Underworld of Kerberos—not to the Underworld of Earth. The Underworld of Kerberos was worse than the deepest pits of Tartarus.

I couldn't let Blake end up in Kerberos. The Oracle had to have another option for us. She just *had* to.

But if she didn't... what would we do then?

I had to stop worrying about it. I needed to think about everything one step at a time. Right now, my focus had to be on speaking to the Oracle and getting an answer.

But it was impossible to relax, and as we rolled down the river, my mind was on an endless loop of worrying about the future.

Our boat turned a corner, and the appearance of a gigantic, three-headed dog straight ahead snapped me back into focus. The dog towered over the river, its paws on both sides so its body created a bridge over-head, its yellow eyes staring down at us. It sniffed as we moved closer, lips pulled back as it growled.

Charon rowed us closer and closer to the monstrous beast, and I glanced back at him and Persephone in alarm. Neither of them looked concerned in the slightest.

"Aren't we going to stop before we get too close to that monster?" I asked them, scooting as far back in the boat as possible.

"That monster is Cerberus," Blake said, pulling his sword out and raising it to fight. "The guard of the Gates of the Underworld. We can't get into the Under-world without passing him."

"That's true," Persephone said. "But you need to put away your weapon."

Blake looked back at her like she was crazy, his sword still up and ready to fight.

"I am the Queen of the Underworld," the goddess

reminded us. "Cerberus answers to me. And I command you to put down your weapon. Having it out will accomplish nothing but antagonizing the dog."

Blake glanced back at Cerberus, and after a few more seconds, he reluctantly sheathed his sword.

Now that we were closer, I saw collars around Cerberus's three necks, each one connected to chains that bound him to the Gates. He pulled on the chains, but they didn't budge. And despite Persephone's claims that the dog listened to her, his growling and salivating hadn't stopped. I didn't think she would lie to us... but why was Cerberus still looking at us like he wanted to kill us?

Then Persephone pulled something out of her pocket—three pieces of lotus fruit. I recognized the cherry-sized fruit from the time I'd spent on the Land of the Lotus Eaters a few weeks ago during our quest through Greece. She held the fruit up, and all three of Cerberus's heads stared at them and sniffed. His eyes glazed over at the smell of the snack.

"Sit," Persephone commanded, her voice stern.

Cerberus plopped his butt on the ground. His tongues lolled out of his mouths as he panted in antici-pation of the treat, dog breath invading the air so strongly that I held my hand to my nose to avoid inhaling the stench. His giant tail wagged with so much force that I could feel the breeze on my face.

Charon docked the ferry on the side of the river, and Persephone tossed the pieces of fruit up at the dog. His mouths caught them easily. Once all three heads finished eating, he lay down and closed his eyes, snoring in seconds.

"Works every time." Persephone smiled and hopped off the ferry, wiping her hands on the sides of her dress. "Dogs are much more sensitive to lotus fruit than humans."

Blake and I followed Persephone off the boat, tip-toeing around the sleeping dog until we were gazing up at the towering gates of the Underworld. A shiver passed through my spine at the sight of them. They were black iron, twisted and warped, and as tall as a house. Beyond them was a brown, mountainous waste-land. There was no sun or moon—only a dim tawny light blanketing the area, as if the entire realm was perpetually in a gloomy, cloudy day.

"Don't look so depressed," Persephone said. "The Underworld is not as awful as it initially seems." She stepped up to the gates, and as if they sensed her pres-ence, they creaked open to let us in. She walked through, and having no other option, Blake and I followed her lead.

Once we were far enough inside, the gates slammed shut behind us.

I whipped my head around and stared back at them

in panic. Even though Persephone had sworn on Zeus that she would return us to Earth, I felt trapped. What if something went wrong? What if we ended up stuck here forever? I used to be comforted by the idea of the afterlife, but *this* wasn't what I'd imagined. Now that I was seeing what came next, I never wanted to return here again.

"What now?" Blake asked, zeroing in on Persephone. "When can we speak to Hades?"

"Normally, souls that enter the gate must follow the path up the mountain," Persephone said, pointing to the tallest mountain in the distance. "Once they reach the top, they face the Judges, who place them in an appropriate realm of the Underworld. But you are not dead, so you are not here to be judged... yet. And now that we've entered the realm where I'm Queen, I can access my full powers and transport you to the palace."

"Great." I looked around the barren land surrounding us, wondering if the palace would be just as depressing. "But how are we getting there? Didn't you say that portals can't be created in the Underworld?"

"Just take my hand and close your eyes," she said, holding out her hands for us to take. "I'll take care of the rest."

CHAPTER FORTY-TWO

I reached for her hand, and the moment I closed my
eyes, a comforting warmth filled my body. Everything that had been weighing me down vanished. I was
floating, nowhere and everywhere at once, and I wished
I could remain that way forever.

Seconds later, the warmth vanished, and my feet
were on solid ground again.

"Open your eyes," Persephone told us. "We have
arrived."

I did as she said, and my mouth dropped in awe at
the beauty of the room around me. Hardwood floors,
plush rugs, gold-paneled walls displaying magnificent
artwork, tall carved ceilings, a burning fireplace, a
dazzling chandelier, and colorful antique furniture fit

for a queen—including a grand piano. Floor to ceiling windows lined the far wall, their curtains drawn.

Persephone clapped her hands twice, and the curtains opened, revealing the bluest lake and the clearest sky that I'd ever seen. Bright flowers and trees bursting with fruit surrounded the lake—if I didn't know any better, I would think I was gazing upon Eden itself.

Blake was also taking it all in, looking equally impressed.

"Where are we?" I asked Persephone, because surely we weren't in the Underworld anymore.

"We're in my sitting room in the palace," she said. "Hades is not expecting visitors—he doesn't even expect *me* to return until the fall equinox. Since my chambers are empty during my six months on Earth, I thought this would be the safest place to arrive so we didn't take anyone by surprise."

"It's beautiful." I ran my fingers along a nearby end table—there was no dust on it at all. "But... are we really still in the Underworld? It looks nothing like where we first arrived."

"Yes, we're still in the Underworld." Persephone laughed. "My chambers overlook the Crystal Lake in Elysium. Hades wanted me to be comfortable in my home here, so he ensured that my rooms overlooked the lake. It's the best view in the entire palace. Better than even the view from his own rooms."

"That was kind of him," I said, although I was surprised, since kindness wasn't a trait I expected from Hades. "So, Elysium is a part of the Underworld?"

"There are four realms in the Underworld," Persephone explained. "Think of the realms like continents. As I mentioned earlier, all souls that enter the Underworld must face the Judges, who place them in an appropriate realm. Tartarus is for the worst of the worst, the Fields of Punishment is for those who broke the law and committed crimes in their life, Asphodel Meadows is for those who were ordinary and mediocre, and Elysium is for the heroic souls who achieved greatness in their lives —especially those who are related to the gods."

"So Chris might be in Elysium?" Blake asked, and I swallowed down tears at the mention of his name.

"I'm not supposed to tell you this..." She stepped closer to us, glanced around the room, and lowered her voice, as if letting us in on a huge secret. "But I have it on good authority that Chris *is* in Elysium. Hypatia is there as well. Their heroic actions saved the world from Typhon. The decision to send them to Elysium was an easy one, and they're incredibly deserving of their places there."

"Thank you," I told her. "For telling me. It means a

lot." I wiped away a tear and looked back out at the lake. "Do you think we might see them out there?"

"Elysium is a large realm," she said. "Not as large as Asphodel Meadows and the Fields of Punishment, but it's larger than any continent on Earth. You will not see them while you're here. But you're a daughter of Apollo. Continue on the path you're on now, and you'll surely join them in Elysium when your time comes."

"It looks like a great place to be," Blake said, joining me at the window. "I'm glad I'm here to see it now."

I opened my mouth to add that he would end up in Elysium as well, since he's also a descendant of the gods, but then I closed it. Because if Blake sacrificed himself to Kerberos, he *couldn't* end up in the Underworld of Earth. He would end up in the Underworld of Kerberos.

In the Underworld of Kerberos, nothing like Elysium existed. It was eternal Hell for everyone.

"Hopefully we can speak with Hades as soon as possible," I told Persephone, since the sooner we spoke to Hades, the sooner we would be able to speak to the Oracle. "When can you tell him that we're here?"

"Right now," she answered. "I'll go find him. Once he's ready, I'll retrieve you from here and escort you to his throne room."

She closed her eyes, and in a burst of warm light, she was gone.

CHAPTER FORTY-THREE

S ilence descended upon the room after Persephone disappeared. It was so strange. For the first time since we'd officially started dating, I had no idea what to say to Blake.

So I walked across the room and sat down at the piano, laying my fingers on the keys and starting to play. This was the most exquisite piano I'd ever seen in person, and the melody flowed from my body—my favorite song from the musical *The Phantom of the Opera*. It was the show my mom had starred in back in college—the show that Apollo had attended, when he'd heard my mom sing for the first time.

It was crazy to think that if he hadn't attended the show that night—if he hadn't heard my mom sing and spoken to her as she left through the stage door—I never would have been born.

Now, I cleared my mind, thinking only of the music. For the past few months, all I'd been doing was training and fighting. But music was in my blood, too, and sitting at the piano, letting the notes flow from my body, made me feel more relaxed than I'd been in weeks.

Once I finished the song, Blake sat down next to me on the bench, the side of his body pressing against mine. "That was beautiful," he told me, his eyes soft and intense. "Once this is all over, I hope you have time to play piano more often."

"Thanks." I pulled my fingers off the keys and turned away from him. Because after all of this, if I *did* play piano more often, he wouldn't be there to hear it.

With Blake gone, I feared that the music in my soul would be gone, too.

But before either of us could say another word, Persephone appeared in the middle of the room. She'd changed out of her green dress—now she was wearing a red velvet gown with a cinched waist and a low neckline.

"I've told Hades that you're here," she told us, holding her hands out for us to take. "He's ready to speak with you, and he's waiting in the throne room."

CHAPTER FORTY-FOUR

W e took Persephone's hands, and she teleported us into a room much larger and more intimidating than her sitting room—the royal throne room.

Looking around, I felt like I'd traveled back in time to medieval Europe. The ceiling was as tall as the one in the New Alexandrian Library, and it was held up by thick columns and curving archways. The room was dark, lit up only by torches that lined the walls, and two stone fountains bursting with fire instead of water. Red carpet rolled down the room and up the steep steps, leading up to two magnificent thrones.

A handsome man with jet-black hair, wearing dark jeans and a black leather jacket, already occupied one throne. He had the chiseled look of a classic star from the early days of Hollywood. But his skin was as pale as a ghost's, as if he was dead himself.

I assumed he was Hades.

Persephone glided up the steps and took the throne next to him, falling naturally into her seat by his side. But with her tan skin and red dress, she looked so *alive* next to him. Almost as if she were out of place in the Underworld itself.

I waited for one of them to speak, but they both stared at us, saying nothing.

Were we supposed to kneel? Bow to them? It would have been nice if Persephone had given us a heads-up about the protocol before dropping us at the foot of Hades's throne. Now I just shuffled my feet, my eyes darting around as I searched for a hint about how to proceed.

Blake glanced over at me, gave me a reassuring nod, and walked to the bottom of the steps. I tried to remain steady as I followed him, hoping my nerves didn't show.

"I'm Blake Carter, descendant of Ares and wielder of fire," he said, the fire in the fountains blazing higher as he spoke. "And this is Nicole Cassidy, daughter of Apollo and conductor of spirit."

"I know who you are." Hades held his gaze with ours, his voice steady and low. "And I'd like to know what you need to ask me that was important enough for my wife to bring you here during the months she's free to spend up on Earth."

"How much do you know about the threat of the portal to Kerberos opening and the Titans returning to Earth?" I asked him.

"I may live in the Underworld, but I'm not completely cut off from Earth," he said. "I know about you and the other Elementals, and I know of your recent feat of defeating the monsters that have escaped from Kerberos, including Typhon himself. Impressive achievements, I must say."

"Thank you," I said, my cheeks flushing at having been complimented by a god.

"However, I wasn't expecting to meet you until your mortal bodies passed on and your souls joined those of the other heroes in Elysium," he continued. "I assume that for my wife to have broken protocol and transported you here now, that you need something from me of much importance."

"Yes." I nodded. "We do."

"Then get on with it," he said. "I don't have all day."

Persephone said nothing from her throne next to him, although she did give me a small nod, encouraging me to continue.

"You just said that you expect to see all of us Elementals in Elysium once we officially arrive in the Underworld," I said, his recent statement giving me the idea to approach it from this angle. "So as the King of the Underworld, I assume you feel it's of utmost importance that every soul goes to its proper realm after death."

"I do," he confirmed.

"So do I," I said, pausing to emphasize that Hades and I agreed on that key point. "But Nyx told us that the only way to seal the portal to Kerberos is for either Blake or Danielle to bind it from the Kerberos side. Once they do that, they'll be stuck in Kerberos forever. And if they die in Kerberos... they'll end up in the Underworld there, serving an eternity in an afterlife that they don't deserve. I was hoping you could help us make sure that doesn't happen."

"I see how that's problematic," Hades said, rubbing his chin with his thumb. "But I don't think there's anything I can do to help. The portal needs to be closed —if it isn't, the consequences will be deadly for everyone on Earth *and* in the Underworld. If Nyx told you that that's the only way to seal the portal, then she's telling the truth."

"And I'm prepared to make that sacrifice," Blake said, the reminder ripping my heart into pieces all over again. "Unless there's another way to seal the portal that even Nyx doesn't know about."

"Nyx is an ancient primordial deity—older than all

but Chaos himself," Hades said. "If there were another way to close the portal, she would tell you."

"Unless there's another way that even *she* doesn't know about," I said, narrowing my eyes in challenge.

Hades raised his eyebrows—I'd clearly piqued his interest. "And who, young demigod, do you think knows more about the Universe than Nyx?" he asked.

"The only person in all of history who can clearly see the exact future." I held his gaze, each word coming out strong and confident. "The Oracle herself."

CHAPTER FORTY-FIVE

"Ah." Hades nodded, giving us a knowing smile. "I see now why you ventured down to the Underworld. You think the Oracle will tell you something that Nyx couldn't."

"We think it's a possibility," Blake said. "We don't have many options—this seemed like it had the best chance of working. Because if there's another way to close the portal, the Oracle would know, right?"

"She would," Hades said. "But when the Oracle was alive, she was merely a mortal. Now she's a spirit living out her afterlife in Elysium. She can still see the future, but going to her with this question could be an insult to Nyx herself. And as I understand it, Nyx has watched out for you and supported you throughout your entire journey. Do you truly wish to risk insulting Nyx by questioning her knowledge?"

"We're not questioning her knowledge," I said. "I trust that Nyx is being honest with us about what she knows. But if the Oracle knows something more... I just couldn't live with myself if we left any possible stone unturned."

"I understand that you see it that way." His eyes were far off, and I could practically see the wheels in his brain spinning. "However, Nyx might see it differently."

"Then that's a risk we're willing to take," Blake said.

"*You* might be willing to take it," Hades said. "But am I?"

"It's just one question," I begged. "Let us see the Oracle, and I promise you won't see us again until our souls come to the Underworld to live out our afterlives."

A shadow passed over Hades's eyes, and I feared he was about to say no.

"This is too complicated of a decision to make on a whim," Persephone finally spoke up. She turned to Hades, her gaze soft and loving, and placed her hand on top of his. "Perhaps we should sleep on it and come to a decision in the morning?"

"You'll stay here tonight even though it's one of the months that you're allowed on Earth?" He watched her carefully, waiting for her response.

"Yes." She rearranged her hair so it perfectly framed her face, and her lips curved up into a small smile. "I'll show Blake and Nicole their accommodation, and then I'll meet you in our room."

"Very well." He nodded to her and looked back at us. "I'll send Persephone to find the two of you in the morning, and she'll bring you to me so I can inform you of my decision."

And then, without waiting to see our reaction, he disappeared.

CHAPTER FORTY-SIX

"I would walk you to your room so you could see more of the palace, but it's best that I don't lose any time that I could be spending with Hades," Persephone said, holding out her hands for us to take. "Come. I'll make sure you're situated in your room, and then I'll come get you in the morning, once Hades has reached a decision."

We took her hands, and she teleported us to our room.

I opened my eyes to the sight of a huge canopy bed with a red comforter that looked as soft as velvet. Fit for royalty, the bed was magnificently carved, as were the nightstands, chairs, and tables. I turned and saw a buffet spread across the wall near the glowing fireplace, with food and drink ready for us to eat. It smelled delicious, and my stomach growled, reminding me that it had been a long time since my last meal.

But I kept glancing back at the bed. Because despite its size, there was only *one* bed.

Warmth rushed to my cheeks, and I wrung my hands together, unable to look at Blake. We'd never spent the night together before. In fact, I'd never shared a bed with a guy—ever. Perhaps I should have asked for my own room?

But I didn't want to sleep alone in Hades's castle, and despite how upset I'd been at Blake since he'd volunteered to sacrifice himself to Kerberos, I trusted him.

So despite my trepidations, I said nothing.

"There are night clothes in the dresser, and a private bathroom through that door," Persephone said, pointing to each of them. "I hope these accommodations will do. It's rare that we have visitors, but apart from Hades's room and my room, this is the nicest in the castle."

"It's beautiful," I assured her, since it was. "And thank you for doing all of this for us. I don't know why you're helping us, but I really do appreciate it. Without your help..." I glanced at Blake, unable to say more without risking bursting into tears, and turned back to Persephone. "I'm just glad we might be able to learn about another option."

"I'm happy to help." Persephone walked to the buffet and picked up a pomegranate, looking down at it sadly. "I respect Hades very much, and after all the time I've been forced to spend with him here in the Underworld, I do love him as a partner and as a co-ruler," she said, lifting her gaze to look back at us. "But I'm not *in* love with him. I never have been, and I don't think I ever will be." She took a deep breath, replacing her melancholy expression with a small smile. "Like the other Olympians, I've been following your adventures since the night of the comet. So much hinges on your closing the portal. And as an observer, I've also witnessed the love between the two of you. Your love may still be blooming, but it's the type of love I always wished I had myself. I'll never have it, so it's my pleasure to do everything in my power to assist you in your quest to not be separated for all eternity."

"You're able to see what's happening on Earth from the Underworld?" Blake asked her.

"Yes." Persephone nodded. "Hades knew how much I missed my family during the six months I'm required to spend here every year, so centuries ago, he provided me with a mirror that allows me to watch what's happening on Earth. It's a one-way mirror, so those I'm watching can't see me, but it's better than not being able to see them at all. It helps make my time here more bearable."

"That was kind of him," I said. "He seems to care about you a lot."

"He does," she agreed, placing the pomegranate back down with the other fruit. "But love—*true* love—can't be forced. It either exists or it doesn't. It's rare to find love that's true, and even if someday I *did* find it, I can't see how it would work out given my current situation. So I make the best with what I have. And helping others —especially two young people in love—makes me happy. *That's* why I'm helping you."

"Thank you," I told her. "I'm not sure what I could ever offer of equal value that you would want, but someday in the future, I hope I'll be able to repay you."

"Please don't feel as if you owe me." She brushed the idea away as if it were silly and headed to the door, resting her hand on the knob. "Now, before I take leave, is there anything else you need?"

"Not that I can think of," Blake said. "But I do have one last question."

CHAPTER FORTY-SEVEN

"Yes?" Persephone watched him closely, waiting for him to continue.

"This food looks delicious," he said, motioning to the buffet. "But I've been studying Greek mythology for as long as I remember. An important rule I learned is not to eat or drink anything while in the Underworld. Doing so can get a person stuck down here forever, just like what happened to you when you ate the six pomegranate seeds and were forced to spend six months of every year here because of it." He glanced at the fruit that she'd picked up earlier. "Will the same thing happen to us if we eat or drink anything laid out for us tonight?"

"I swore upon Zeus that I would return you to Earth when you request that I do so," she said. "That oath supersedes the law that those who eat in the Under-world must stay in the Underworld. Plus—I am the Queen. If I wish to break the law, then the law will be broken. So please, eat. It wouldn't do to have you go hungry while you're here."

"Thank you," I said, and relief washed over me, since I *was* starving, and the food looked delicious.

"Now, Hades is waiting for me, so I will take my leave," Persephone said. "I will see you in the morning."

A warm light surrounded her, and she was gone.

"So…" I looked around awkwardly, not knowing what to do. Blake and I hadn't been alone for longer than ten minutes since he'd volunteered to bind the portal from Kerberos. I was still processing my feelings about it all —and I was so hurt that I didn't even know where to start.

Instead, I walked to the buffet and opened one of the silver containers, my stomach growling at the sight and smell of my all-time favorite food—pizza.

"The pizza's half pepperoni and half pineapple," I said with a smile, since we had an ongoing joke about how I didn't understand how he could possibly enjoy pineapple on pizza. I opened up the other containers, pleased to find more of my favorite foods—grilled cheese, tacos, mini-hamburgers, and macaroni and cheese. There was way more than two people could possibly eat, but I put one of each on my plate and sat down at the table, wanting to try it all.

"Do you want red or white?" Blake asked from the buffet.

"Red or white what?" I asked.

"Wine." He smirked. "They've left both options for us. I guess there's no drinking age in the Underworld."

"I guess not," I agreed. "But... I've never actually had wine before. The only drinks I've ever had are beer and mixed liquor drinks at parties, and to be honest, I've never liked the taste."

"That's because people buy the cheap stuff for parties," he said. "Not liking that shows you have *good* taste. But these wines are in a decanter, which aerates the finest wines so they're ready to drink. I think it's safe to assume that the King and Queen of the Underworld spared no expense."

"Which do you prefer?" I asked.

"For tonight?" His eyes softened, and my heart flip-flopped all the way from my stomach into my throat. "Red. Definitely red."

"Okay," I said, my voice catching in my throat. "But only a little. I don't want to get drunk."

"Witches have a naturally high alcohol tolerance," he told me. "And you're a demigod—yours is probably higher than ours. One glass of wine won't get you drunk. It won't even get you tipsy."

I nodded, since I supposed that made sense. Back in Georgia, I'd gone to a few parties where there was alcohol. Some of the girls acted silly after only one beer. They'd claimed it was because of the alcohol, but I could barely feel a thing, so I assumed they were acting drunk to get attention. They convinced me to have one more beer to see if I felt it, and it didn't work. I just felt gross from all the liquid sloshing around in my stomach.

That was the end of my adventures with drinking... but at least now I knew that if I enjoyed the wine, one glass wouldn't hurt.

Blake brought a plate of food to the table—he'd taken even more than me—and then he went back to pour the wine, bringing back one for each of us. He sat down to join me and raised his glass in the air. I followed his lead and raised mine as well.

"To getting an answer from the Oracle tomorrow," he said, his gaze locked on mine.

"To getting an answer that we *want*," I clarified, clinking my glass with his. Then I lifted the glass to my lips and took a small sip, smiling at the burst of flavor on my tongue.

"You like it?" He cocked his head to the side, waiting for my answer.

"Yes." I took a full sip this time to fully enjoy the flavor. "I do."

It had been nearly an entire day since our last meal, so we dug into our food, barely speaking as we ate. It was the best food I'd ever had. I wondered if Hades and Persephone had hired the best chefs of all time to make it for us. It was possible, since they had every dead person in the world accessible to them. I doubted that any other meal I would have in my life would compare.

I came close to finishing everything on my plate, but it was so much food that I eventually dropped the final half of my cheeseburger down in defeat.

Blake raised an eyebrow at my nearly empty plate. "I guess you won't have room for dessert?" he asked.

"No way." I shook my head, scrunching my nose at the thought of fitting any more food into my stomach.

But then my thoughts went back to Blake—mainly, about what he would have to endure in Kerberos. Because in Kerberos, the food was dangerous. I didn't know what it would do to him, because Erebus had ensured that we had enough power bars to keep us going through our journey, but I had no doubts that the effects of the food there would be horrible.

And Blake would be forced to endure it for all eternity.

"What's wrong?" He reached forward to rest his hand on top of mine, but I pulled away, bringing mine back down to my lap. Not because I didn't want to hold his hand—I did, more than I could say. But because I was afraid that if he touched me right now, I wouldn't be able to stop myself from bursting into tears.

I didn't want him to see me weak like that—not when he was being so strong.

"It's just been a long day," I said, pushing back my chair and standing up. "I'm going to go shower."

I rushed to the bathroom without waiting for his response, got into the shower, and finally allowed the tears to fall.

CHAPTER FORTY-EIGHT

I stayed in the shower for a while, crying until my tear ducts were so dried out that crying any more was impossible. I once had a science teacher who said that when people cried, the sadness in our brains was an actual chemical that transferred out of our bodies through our tears. If that were true, crying was supposed to make me feel *better*.

But my heart felt just as crushed as it did before.

By coming to the Underworld, I was doing everything I could to make it so Blake didn't have to sacrifice himself to Kerberos. But I wouldn't be able to feel better until the Oracle gave us another solution to the challenge ahead. I doubted I would sleep well tonight, but if I *tried* to fall asleep, then tomorrow—and the answers it would bring—would come faster. So I turned off the water and got out of the shower, hoping I didn't look like a *complete* wreck after my crying session.

I'd bolted to the shower so quickly that I hadn't bothered to take pajamas into the bathroom with me, so I wrapped myself in a towel, brushed out my hair, and walked back into the bedroom. My eyes met with Blake's, and I held the towel closer, feeling practically naked there in front of him. I was sure in that moment that he could see straight into my soul, and every inch of my body ached to run up to him and kiss him and pretend that everything was going to be all right and that he would be able to live out the rest of his life on Earth.

Instead, I just stood there, my gaze locked with his, saying nothing. What could I possibly say that wouldn't result in me breaking down into tears again?

"I'm going to jump in the shower, too," he said, finally breaking the silence. "You can get changed while I'm in there."

I nodded, watching him as he walked into the bathroom and closed the door behind him. Once the shower was running, I opened the wardrobe and gasped. Because the doors opened to reveal a hidden walk-in closet and dressing room that was nearly the size of my bedroom at home.

I stepped in, closed the door behind me, and

perused what was available. There were gowns on the female side and tuxedos on the male side. It looked like a closet for nobility in the time of Victorian England. My appearance today had been the last thing on my mind, but Hades must have thought that Blake and I looked a mess in the throne room in our jeans and t-shirts. I hoped it hadn't negatively influenced his decision.

I searched my side of the closet for pajamas, finding only a selection of lacy, silk, or see-through night-gowns. They were nothing like what I normally wore to bed at home—shorts or sweatpants with a tank top. But with no other option, I found a sort-of modest black silk one and slipped it on, turning to see how it looked in the full-length mirror.

It fell to the top of my thighs, showing more leg than I would ever reveal in public. But at least the material wasn't sheer, so I didn't feel completely exposed. If my eyes didn't feel so puffy from crying, and if they didn't have dark circles under them from exhaustion, I might even think I looked pretty. As it was, I felt like a mess— both inside and out.

I was so tired that it was tempting to get into bed, bury myself under the comforter, and fall asleep. But I couldn't go to sleep without seeing Blake. Because—as much as I hated to remind myself of it—I didn't know how much time I had left with him. I had to at least talk to him and see if there was anything I could say that would get him to change his mind about his decision. If I didn't say or do everything in my power to try to convince him to change his mind, I would never be able to forgive myself.

I wasn't sure what I *could* say, but I had to try.

With nothing else to do but wait, I slipped on a pair of fluffy slippers, picked up my glass of wine, and curled up in the armchair facing the fireplace. Our plates had been cleared and the food had miraculously disappeared while Blake was in the shower and I was in the closet. All that remained was a decanter of red wine, and a selection of cookies, chocolates, and pastries. But I still wasn't hungry, so I sipped my wine, getting lost in my thoughts as I stared into the fire, which was burning smaller and smaller as time passed.

Suddenly, the flames flared back to life, so high that they licked the top of the mantle. I turned around and saw Blake standing near the door, a satisfied smirk on his face. He wore black silk pajama pants, but none of the shirts in the wardrobe must have been to his liking, because his top was bare, showing off his tanned, chiseled chest. His hair was still wet from the shower.

He picked up his glass of wine and sat down in the armchair next to mine. His eyes roamed the length of my body, and heat rose to my cheeks under his gaze.

"I was curious about which nightgown you would

choose," he said, the light of the flames dancing across his face. "You look beautiful."

"Thanks." I glanced down at the nightgown again and straightened, feeling less self-conscious about it now. "That closet was... something else."

"It was." He nodded, and we sat together in silence for a few seconds, sipping our wine.

I stared into my drink, unsure what to say next. There was so much on my mind. Where was I supposed to start?

"I hate this wall between us," he finally said, breaking the silence. "It's been there since we spoke to Nyx last night. I know you're not happy about my decision... but I wish you would talk to me about it."

"You volunteered to leave me *forever*." I snapped my head up to look at him, my eyes hot with tears and anger. "You didn't take time to think about it. You didn't ask me what *I* thought about it. Because how am I supposed to get through every day without you, knowing that you're going through hell on the other side of that portal—or that you could be stuck in the hellish Underworld there forever? I don't think I can do it. I *know* I can't." The tears flowed freely down my cheeks again, and despite my attempts to wipe them away, they wouldn't stop. I didn't think I *wanted* them to stop.

"Of course you can." He got up and joined me in my

chair, pulling me to his chest and wrapping his arms around me. "I love you, Nicole," he said, his voice full of so much strength and passion that I knew he meant it. "And it's *because* I love you that I have to do this. If I don't, then you'll never be safe. *No one* on Earth will ever be safe. I couldn't live with myself if I let that happen."

"It didn't have to be you." I snuggled closer into him, resting my cheek against his chest. In his arms, I felt so warm and safe. I wished we could stay here in this moment forever. "It could have been... someone else."

"You mean Danielle." He said it as a statement, not a question.

"Yeah." I sniffed. "Not that I want it to be *either* of you. But you didn't even wait to see what she would say."

"I've known Danielle for my entire life," he said. "She's smart, she fights for the people she cares for, and she goes for what she wants no matter what. But she's selfish. She would never volunteer herself. It had to be me. I knew it had to be me the moment Nyx told us what we needed to do. And I think, deep down, you know it, too."

"I don't know." I shrugged, not wanting to admit it. "But it's not fair. I just got you back. You have no idea what it was like... you were *dead*, Blake. I saw your body. Your *corpse*. In that moment, believing I would never be able to see you again... everything in me shattered. But now you're back. You're here. You're *alive*. And I refuse to believe that I got you back only to lose you again so quickly. The world can't be that cruel."

"It might not have to happen that way," he said. "The Oracle could have the answer."

"She might," I said. "Or she might not. If she doesn't, then you'll be gone. Forever. I already had to go through that once... I can't do it again."

"Is that why you've been distancing yourself from me this past day?" he asked. "Because you think you're going to lose me again?"

"Yes." I turned my head up to look at him, gazing into his eyes. "The thought of losing you—of what you're inflicting on yourself by trapping yourself in Kerberos—it absolutely terrifies me."

"It scares me, too," he admitted. "But if I don't do it, the world will end because I was too scared to do anything about it. I couldn't live with that. We've risked our own lives enough these past few weeks that you have to understand that. Right?"

"There has to be another way," I said, refusing to answer his question. "There just *has* to."

"If there is, we'll do everything in our power to discover it," he said. "But no matter what, never doubt how much I love you. I came with you down to the *Underworld* to try to find another solution to this problem. I will go with you anywhere if it means we'll have a chance at a future together. No matter what happens, I hope you never forget that."

"I love you, too." I trailed my thumb over his cheek, trying to commit every inch of his face to my memory. "Knowing that there's still a possibility—a *big* possibility—that you'll have to make this sacrifice... it hurts more than I can say. But I don't want to distance myself from you. If we only have a limited amount of time left... I want to spend as much of it together as possible."

"I know we haven't been together for that long, but we've been through so much that it feels like forever." His lips were so close to mine now, electricity buzzing between us. "I don't know if I can properly get across how much you mean to me, but we don't know how much time we have left together, so I'm going to try. Because before you, my life was empty and void. I went through the motions, but I wasn't fully *there*. Then you burst into my life with fire and passion and lit it up in ways I never thought possible. With you, I feel more alive than ever. I've told you a million times, but I'll say it once more—I love you, Nicole. I don't want you to ever doubt that. So tonight—if you're ready—I want us to be together completely. I want to show you how deep my love for you goes."

Tears filled my eyes, and I nodded, my heart fuller

than it had been in my entire life. "Yes," I said, and I crushed my lips to his, running my fingers up his chest and burying them in his hair. A moan sounded from deep in my throat, and I arched my body up, pushing it hard against his. But it wasn't close enough. Every inch of me pulsed with desire for Blake. I wanted *more*. I wanted *him*.

And I told him just that.

So he picked me up and carried me to the bed, and that night, we loved each other more than we ever had before.

CHAPTER FORTY-NINE

The next morning, a knock on the door jolted me out of my sleep.

My eyes opened, and Blake's eyes staring back at me were the first things I saw. I smiled at the memory of last night and snuggled closer into him. We'd been holding each other all night, and I'd never slept better. Being with him, with his arms around me, it just made me feel so... safe.

The knocking started again, and my cheeks turned red at the realization that neither Blake nor I were wearing any clothes. They'd been removed and flung across the floor pretty quickly last night. But at least whoever was outside the door hadn't taken the liberty of letting themselves in. If they had, they would have seen a *lot* more than they'd bargained for.

"One minute!" Blake yelled to them, and we both scurried around the room, throwing on the clothes we'd worn yesterday. They were rumpled and dirty from the journey to the Underworld, but since my only other choices in that closet were barely-there night-gowns or fancy dresses, they would have to do.

Once we were both dressed, Blake told the person on the other side of the door that they could come in.

Persephone glided inside, wearing a long lilac dress that flowed behind her. Her hair was down and in waves, her cheeks were flushed pink, and her eyes were so bright that she looked like she'd already been awake for hours.

"The Oracle warned me not to teleport directly into your room," she said with a knowing smile. "Not that I would have anyway—for privacy's sake."

"The Oracle?" My jaw dropped open—I was too happy to hear that Persephone had spoken with the Oracle to be embarrassed that she knew what had been going on in the bedroom between Blake and me. "You spoke with her?"

"I have." She nodded. "She's waiting for you in the throne room. And she said not to worry about your apparel—the jeans and t-shirts you're wearing now are perfectly acceptable to her."

But even though it was happy news, I noticed a falter in Persephone's chipper appearance, and sadness passed over her eyes. She covered it up quickly, but now that I was looking closer, I had a gut feeling that something wasn't right. She looked... defeated.

"What happened?" I asked her. "Why don't you look happy that we get to speak with the Oracle?" I held my breath, bracing myself for the worst. "Is the news bad, but you're not telling us so we can hear it from her ourselves?"

"No, no, nothing of the sort." She waved away the possibility. "The Oracle wouldn't say a word about what she knew until the two of you were present."

"What's wrong then?" I asked. "Something changed since last night. I can tell."

"Well, as you know, Hades wasn't thrilled with the idea of bringing the Oracle here to speak with you." She glanced at the ground, twisting her fingers together. "He views this allowance as not trusting Nyx, and he doesn't want to offend the primordial deities. But I think the Oracle is the best chance in finding the answer you seek, so I bargained on your behalf."

"What did you bargain?" I asked, my heart dropping at the possibilities.

"Hades has allowed you to speak with the Oracle... in exchange to my agreeing to spend one extra month with him in the Underworld each year."

"What?" My eyes bulged at her confession. "But you

don't like it down here. Why would you offer to do that?"

"I am used to it down here," she answered flatly. "I was born above, and will always miss Earth and my family there. But as centuries have passed, I've realized that my place is here, as the Queen of the Underworld. I have more to offer here than I do on Earth. The transition was going to happen sooner or later, and if I could use it as a bargaining chip to benefit the two of you in your quest, then that makes it all the better."

My heart dropped at what she'd given up. But it was already done. And knowing what I did about bargains and oaths made by gods, there would be no taking it back.

"Thank you." I bowed my head to her, wanting her to know that her sacrifice was appreciated. "I will not forget what you've done for us today."

"I only hope that the Oracle has the information you seek." She held her hands out, motioning for us to take them. "Come. We shall not keep her waiting any longer."

Blake and I took her hands, and I closed my eyes, warmth filling my body as Persephone transported us to the Oracle.

CHAPTER FIFTY

Wе appeared at the base of the steps in the throne room.

Hades sat upon his throne, and Persephone walked up to take her seat beside him. In between them was a woman wearing a simple gray habit, with a matching hood that hid her hair and eyes. She looked like a nun. All I could see of her was the bottom of her face—her nose and mouth.

"The two of you have a question you wish to ask me?" She faced our direction and pressed her palms together, although with her eyes covered, there was no way she could see us.

"You are the Oracle," Blake said, clearing his throat. "Surely you already know what we want to ask?"

I glared at him, resisting the urge to elbow him in the side for being snarky to the Oracle.

"Clever." She chuckled, and I relaxed, glad she wasn't offended. "I suppose it might have been funny the first time I heard it thousands of years ago, although with so many visions of the future swarming my mind, it gets rather difficult to recall the past." She stopped laughing and stood straighter, turning serious again. "Of course, I *do* know what you wish to know. But I ask you to pose the question to me because there are many ways that a person can word their desires. Oftentimes, one does not understand exactly what he or she truly wants until the words are spoken out loud."

"Okay." I stared straight up at her, even though it was impossible to see her eyes. "Is there another way to seal the portal to Kerberos that doesn't involve anyone sacrificing themselves and getting stuck there?"

She remained standing there with her hands pressed together, silent. I could barely breathe. I could barely *think*. Whatever she said would let me know if I had a future with Blake or not.

The anxiety made me dizzy, and I reached for Blake's hand, steadying myself the moment his fingers wrapped around mine. We were a team. We were stronger together. We loved and supported each other, and there was nothing we couldn't face.

I glanced at Hades and Persephone to see if this pause was normal for the Oracle. They were calm and composed, so I had to assume that it was.

Finally, the Oracle lifted the hood off her face, revealing empty, white eyes. The places where her irises and pupils should have been were blank. Murky. Blind.

I swallowed down a shudder, not wanting to offend her in case she could see me. From the way she looked straight at us, it seemed like she *could*, but the emptiness in her gaze said otherwise.

"Seek alternative answers all you wish, but I will tell you the truth right here—there is no other way to close the portal," she said, her voice slow and hypnotizing. "The way Nyx instructed you is correct, and it is the *only* way to ensure that the Titans don't return to ravage the Earth. You *must* seal the portal in this manner, or else the Titans will return, and everything on Earth—and in the Underworld—will be destroyed."

The floor felt like it dropped out from under me. The only reason I remained standing was because Blake was still holding my hand in his. If his hand left mine, I would surely fall over.

"No," I rasped. "That can't be true. There has to be another way. There *has* to be..." I glanced up at Blake, desperate for him to have some sort of solution. But he looked just as crushed as I felt.

"I'm sorry," the Oracle said. "There is no other way."

And with those few words, any last sliver of hope I had was lost.

CHAPTER FIFTY-ONE

The Oracle was correct that I would seek other answers. For the next two months, that was all the group of us focused on. Not only did we want to find another solution, but having a goal helped keep our minds off of the deaths of Chris and Hypatia. We spoke to every Head Elder, read through as many books as we could in the New Alexandrian Library, and even spoke with a few gods. But the answers were all the same.

There was only one way to close that portal, and it involved either Blake or Danielle sacrificing themselves to Kerberos.

I felt like I was living in a fog. Every day that passed was one day closer to the day that I would lose Blake forever. But despite the Oracle's words, I pressed on, refusing to give up until time ran out.

I'd even tried—multiple times—to speak with Danielle. But talking to her was like talking to a brick wall. She just sat there and listened to my pleas, saying nothing. I wasn't even sure if she was hearing what I was saying, and I certainly wasn't getting through to her.

Unfortunately, I couldn't blame her for shutting me out. I was basically asking her to die instead of Blake. It wasn't right or fair, but I couldn't help it. I *had* to try. I even tried to appeal to the love that she might still have for Blake—after all, they did date for months before I entered the picture. But still, nothing. I had no idea what was going through her mind, and any attempt to find out got me no results.

Eventually I stopped speaking with her altogether, instead spending my time with Blake and Kate as we continued to search for another answer. We'd basically moved into the library by now—it was easier to sleep here than to bother a Head Elder to create a portal for us every time we wanted to go back home. I spent every night with Blake, the two of us growing closer every day. And every day, my heart hurt more and more knowing that I might lose him. But I refused to push him away again. If these were my final weeks with him, I didn't want us to be parted for a single second.

Now we were all sitting around a table in the library, each of us reading a different ancient scroll. We could understand the ones in Greek, thanks to the blood of our Greek god ancestors that ran through our veins, but the ones in other languages were gibberish to us. So we were hoping that we could find *something* in one of the Greek scrolls.

As for Danielle, we had no idea where she was. She'd been disappearing a lot recently. She would never tell us where she went, except to let us know that she was working on figuring out a solution, too. I wasn't sure if she was being honest, but I didn't push her, since I didn't have it in me to speak with her any more than necessary.

But as hard as we tried—and we *did* stay awake for countless hours each night trying—we knew deep in our hearts that it was hopeless. The Oracle couldn't be wrong. Still, at least researching gave us something to do, and a bit of hope.

Hope was the only thing keeping me going right now.

We were buried in the scrolls when our phones all buzzed—a group text from Jason.

More monsters escaped Kerberos. Creating a portal for you in the front of the Library.

We dropped the scrolls, grabbed our weapons, and raced to the front of the library. Danielle came flying in through the back entrance a second later to join us, the Golden Sword in hand. She must have been doing something outside—training, perhaps? There was no point in asking, since she was barely honest with us about anything anymore.

Seconds later, a portal appeared in the middle of the foyer, and we hurried through without hesitation.

I'd traveled through so many portals that led to different spots on Earth that I was used to the temporary darkness, and the feeling of the ground disappearing from under my feet.

My stomach flipped, and then I was standing on solid ground—staring straight at the entrance to the cave as a herd of centaurs stampeded out of it. There were so many of them that the sound of their hooves hitting the ground was deafening. It was already harder than usual to see because it was nighttime, but a cloud of dirt rose up from behind them, making it nearly impossible to make them out.

I coughed as I breathed in the dirt, trying to keep my eyes open despite the pain. There were too many of them to count, but all I knew was that there was *way* more of them than there were of us. And like most of the monsters who'd been escaping recently, the centaurs were strong enough to get past the witches barrier. We simply didn't have the numbers or the power to keep these stronger creatures contained.

Kate cleared away the dirt with her power, and I strung my bow, shooting arrow after arrow at the centaurs. Blake shot fire at them, and Danielle shot icicles, but there were too many of them and they were running too fast for us to get them all. If we charged at them, we would surely be trampled. Kate even created a sinkhole in the ground, which consumed the centaurs near the back of the pack. But too many of the centaurs had already crossed the street into the town, out of range of the sinkhole.

We continued shooting at them—I shot until running out of arrows—but it was no use. Like many of the creatures who had escaped these past few weeks, the centaurs weren't interested in fighting back. They were trying to run *away*. And we didn't have the speed to keep up with them.

The echoing of hooves faded, and I lowered my weapon in defeat. After that loss, more monsters were out in the human world. Every day that the portal remained opened, it was getting weaker, allowing stronger monsters to escape. This was the highest number of them that had gotten through yet.

"Maybe we should seal the portal now and get it over with," Blake said, his eyes empty as he stared at the entrance to the cave.

"No." I shook my head, standing my ground. "We

still have a month until the solstice. We have time to figure out another way."

"I agree with Nicole," Danielle said, surprising me. "After all of this is over, we can go out into the world and hunt down the monsters that escaped. Right now we need as much time as possible to figure out another solution for closing the portal."

"The Oracle's already spoken," Blake reminded us. "We know there's not another way. Which is why our research is leading to *nothing*."

"It's true that the Oracle's already spoken, so I don't know what more we'll be able to find," Kate said, and my heart dropped at how melancholy she sounded. "But I agree with Nicole and Danielle. Blake—we won't let you do this until we've run out of time and explored every possible option. Chris always told us that we're a team, and he's right. We have to do everything in our power to keep each other safe."

And so, with a vote of three against one, Blake conceded, and Jason created another portal for us back to the library to continue our research.

CHAPTER FIFTY-TWO

We were buried in the scrolls the next morning when a portal appeared in the front of the library. I glanced at my phone, but there was no text from Jason. What was going on? He always texted us when he created a portal for us to fight monsters that escaped Kerberos.

I didn't have time to voice my question before someone stepped through the portal—the new Head Elder of Greece himself. He was Hypatia's cousin, and his name was Kostas—we'd met him at her funeral, and later when we questioned the Head Elders to see what they knew about sealing the portal. Like the others, he knew nothing.

Eleven more people followed him, Jason included,

until we were staring at the twelve most powerful Head Elders in the world. Finally, Darius stepped through the portal, a sorrowful look in his eyes as it closed behind him.

Dread pulsed through my body. I had no idea what was happening, but the look in Darius's eyes warned me that we wouldn't like it.

"What's going on?" I stood up and walked over to join them in the atrium. Kate and Blake followed my lead. The sun shined down through the window in the center of the circular ceiling, and I soaked in its rays, taking strength in the light. "What are you all doing here?"

"We need to have a meeting with you." Kostas sized us up, his voice booming through the library. "Where's the water Elemental?"

"I'm right here." Danielle appeared on the balcony, her eyes fierce with determination. I had no idea how she'd heard anything from the study rooms—they were soundproof—but she somehow knew to come out here. She walked down the steps, not faltering in the slightest, and joined us to face the Elders.

"Very well." Kostas nodded. "I'm not sure how long this will take, so the four of you are free to sit down."

"Thanks, but I prefer to stand," Blake said, not budging from his spot. I followed his lead, as did Kate and Danielle. If the Head Elders wanted to meet with us, it would be as equals. They could only intimidate us if we let them.

And I refused to let them.

"As you wish," Kostas said. "In that case, we'll proceed."

"You're the one who came here unannounced and declared this meeting." Blake motioned to Kostas, his gaze strong and unwavering. "The floor's all yours."

Kostas narrowed his eyes at Blake, his lips pressed into a firm line. "As you're aware, dozens of centaurs escaped from Kerberos last night," he began. "You were unable to stop them. And that's on top of all of the other creatures that have managed to escape these past few weeks, while the four of you have been ceaselessly trying to discover an alterative way to seal the portal. However, after what happened last night, it's time to face the hard truth. Both Nyx *and* the Oracle have confirmed that the only way to seal the portal is for either Blake or Danielle to bind it from the Kerberos side. The longer we wait, the more monsters will escape. You need to close the portal now, and seal off Kerberos from Earth forever. It's the only way to keep our world safe. The other Head Elders and I met last night, and they agree with me, which is why we're all here right now."

I stood completely still, the blood draining from my face. Knowing that I would likely lose Blake made my heart hurt more than I could say. I'd been trying to prepare myself for the inevitable... but we were still supposed to have a few weeks together. Those few weeks would give us a chance to figure out another solution. I wasn't ready for this now.

He couldn't make us do this now.

Blake stepped forward, his gaze strong and steady. "I agree with you," he told Kostas, and I sucked in a deep breath, my heart dropping at his words. "We'll close the portal tonight. I'll be the one to bind it from the Kerberos side."

"No," I said, my voice rising in panic. "We can't. Not tonight. We're not ready yet. We need more time..." I stared at him, my eyes begging for him to take it back.

But he refused to even look at me.

"Blake's right." Danielle stepped up to stand next to him, her head held high. "Except he's not going to be the one to bind the portal from the Kerberos side."

"Really?" Kostas raised an eyebrow. "Why is that?"

"Because it's going to be me."

CHAPTER FIFTY-THREE

"What?" I blinked, unable to believe what she'd said. "You're volunteering?"

"Where's this coming from?" Kate asked.

"No." Blake shook his head. "What are you thinking? You can't do that to yourself."

"She can't do it to herself, but you're allowed to do it to *yourself*?" I glared at him, but he just clenched his jaw, saying nothing more.

"I know you're all probably confused." Danielle held her hands up, silencing us. "So instead of bombarding me with questions, let me explain."

"Go ahead." Kostas nodded for her to continue.

Danielle turned around to face all of us, confident and resolved. "I'm sure it hasn't gone unnoticed that for these past few weeks, I've been spending time... elsewhere," she started, and I nodded, since of course we'd all noticed that she'd been distancing herself from the group. "I also hope that you all noticed that while I didn't volunteer until now, I also never refused to be the one to bind the portal from the Kerberos side, either."

I said nothing, since I hadn't noticed that. Not volunteering meant she wasn't volunteering. At least, that's what I'd *thought* it meant.

"Yes," Kate said, surprising me. "I noticed that."

"Thank you," Danielle said to her, appreciation shining in her eyes. "Before I tell you where I've been —and *who* I've been spending that time with—you should know that before coming to a decision, I thought out the practical reasons about who should bind the portal from Kerberos. One reason stood out the most—the fact that Blake can make weapons. He's just starting to discover what he can create, since we've been too distracted with our missions for him to truly see what he can do, but I read the instruction book he received from Nyx in our first treasure hunt around town. It's impressive. Soon he'll be able to create powerful, magical weapons. You're going to need those weapons to defeat the monsters that have escaped Kerberos these past few weeks. And as much as I hate to admit it, that makes me more dispensable than him."

"You're not dispensable," Blake insisted. "None of us are."

"Thank you," she said, and her eyes glimmered with tears. "But you're needed here. And I also know that when I'm in Kerberos, I won't be alone. I'll be protected."

"What do you mean?" I asked.

"*Who* have you been spending all of that time with recently?" Blake narrowed his eyes at Danielle, and I knew him well enough to tell that he suspected what her answer would be.

"Erebus." She glanced down at the floor, her cheeks flushing red. "I don't know if you noticed that when we were in Kerberos, Erebus and I really... connected."

"I noticed," I told her. "It was impossible not to. But I didn't think..." I paused, figuring out how to word this without being offensive. "He's a *primordial deity*. You're a mortal. I thought that once we left Kerberos, that would be it."

"You thought he would forget about me." Danielle said it as a fact, not a question.

"No," I said, although that wasn't completely true, so I shrugged. "I don't know."

"Well, he didn't forget about me," she said. "He *tried* to—but he couldn't."

"I guess you know this because he told you?" Kate asked.

"I didn't see him again until right after Nicole and Blake got back from the Underworld," she continued. "He visited me that night, and he told me that despite trying to forget about me, he couldn't do it. He asked me where I wanted to go most in the world, and I told him Paris, so he took me to the top of the Eiffel Tower. We talked for a while... and then I told him I was thinking of making the sacrifice to Kerberos. Ever since then, he's been taking me everywhere I want to go so that in case I *do* make the sacrifice, I'm able to see the world first."

"Wow," I said. "That explains why you've been gone so much. And how you always appear when we need you. Because *Erebus* knows when we need you, and he brings you back, doesn't he?"

"Yes," she said. "I know this is sudden to you all, but I *love* Erebus. And he loves me. He promised me that if I do end up in Kerberos, he'll stay there with me. He'll keep me protected. He'll even work with me to try to find a way back to Earth. I also won't age while in Kerberos, so we'll be able to search for a long time."

I stared at her, taking this all in. I couldn't believe it. Danielle was actually *volunteering*.

Despite our differences, I didn't like the idea of any of us being stuck in that hell dimension. But Erebus was a primordial deity. He would keep her safe. If there was a way back to Earth, surely he would be able to find it.

And as selfish as I felt for thinking it, I was relieved that Blake didn't have to be the one to close the portal from Kerberos. I wouldn't have to lose him. We would truly have a chance of a future together.

"Have you truly thought this through?" Blake asked Danielle. "You realize that this means you'll never see your family again?"

"I have." She nodded, her eyes sad. "As I'm sure you did, too. Leaving my family isn't something I *want* to do. But if one of us doesn't do this, our families won't be alive for much longer anyway. So really, I'll be *saving* them. I've already written them all letters explaining what I did, for them to read after I leave. They're in my desk in my room."

"I'll make sure the letters get to them," Kate said. "I promise."

"That's *if* Danielle does this and not me," Blake said. "We both volunteered. We still haven't decided which one of us is going."

"Blake..." Danielle said his name softly, focusing only on him. "Even though we're not together anymore, I still love you. I'm not *in* love with you like I am with Erebus, but you're a huge part of my life, and I care about you. In Kerberos, I'll have the protection of a primordial deity who loves me. I'll survive there. You won't. If you do this, it'll be a death sentence. I won't allow that to happen to you."

"You don't know that," he said, his eyes dark and fiery.

"You already died there once," I reminded him, my throat tightening at the memory. "You weren't in Kerberos for long—you don't really know what it's like. We can't use our powers there. You would be a human in a world full of gods and monsters. Yes—you're strong and you're brave—but you're not more powerful than the gods. None of us are."

"And all of those gods and monsters will want to kill you for closing the portal and barring them from Earth forever," Kate added. "It'll be impossible for you to survive that."

"Exactly," Danielle said. "But as a primordial deity, Erebus is stronger than all of those gods and monsters in Kerberos. I'll be safe with him by my side. He was trying hard not to interfere when he was guiding us through the realms there, but Nicole—you saw how he obliterated that dragon. You know he's more than capable of protecting me."

"He is," I said, since everything she was saying made sense. Blake *had* to see it. I looked over at him to see if he agreed, but he was studying Danielle, as if he was trying to get a read on her. He was staring at her like he didn't know her anymore.

"I don't like the idea of *you* going in there any more than you like the idea of *me* going in there," he told her. "And I do trust that Erebus will be able to protect you. But once you're in Kerberos, there's no coming back. So you need to be absolutely sure about this. If you have even a *sliver* of doubt, it's okay. I'll do it. I've been preparing myself for this since the night we spoke with Nyx. I'm ready."

I reached for his hand and squeezed it, aware that despite his brave words, we all knew that Danielle's reasoning made sense. Still, I admired that he was giving her the chance to change her mind. Knowing that he was the type of person to do that cemented my love and respect for him even more.

"There's no changing my mind—I'm going to bind the portal from Kerberos." Danielle looked each of us in the eye, confident and determined, and then turned to face the Head Elders. "And I'm ready to do it right now."

CHAPTER FIFTY-FOUR

T he Head Elders wanted to join us for the ceremony, but we insisted they didn't, since it would be an intense and emotional experience for all of us. After a lot of bickering, they eventually gave in and returned to their homes with the expectation that we would tell them once the portal was sealed, so they could go there and verify that it had been done.

After they left, Jason created a portal to the cave, and Danielle, Kate, Blake, Darius, and I all stepped through. We hadn't actually been *inside* of the cave in weeks, and I was surprised to find that the portal to Kerberos looked different. It was clear enough that we could see through to the other side. When we first saw it months ago, and even up to the time of the equinox, it was dark and muddy. Since then it had been thinning, and it showed in the way it looked, too.

"Are you sure you're ready for this?" Darius asked Danielle.

"I'm as ready as I'll ever be," she said, although she stared at the portal with fear in her eyes. "The Head Elders were clear—we need to close the portal now to keep more monsters from escaping. And even though this isn't easy for me, I agree with them."

"Okay," I said. "As long as it's what you want to do."

"It is." She nodded. "Erebus is there on the other end. He wants to make sure I bind the portal on my own free will, so he's waiting to join me until it's complete. Once it is, he'll stay by my side. Forever."

"From the way he looked at you when we were in Kerberos, I know he will."

Then I did something that I never imagined I would do in a million years—I stepped up to Danielle and hugged her.

She was surprised at first, but she returned the hug.

"Thank you for doing this," I said, pulling away. "Because of you, the world will be safe from the Titans. None of us will forget about your sacrifice here today."

"Wow," Danielle said, managing a small smirk. "From the way you're acting, I might even think that you'll miss me."

"I will," I told her. "Because crazily enough, after all

this time we were forced to spend together, I think we actually became friends."

"I never would have thought it possible when you first moved here, but I guess we did become friends, didn't we?"

We shared a smile, and then I nodded and stepped aside so the others could say their goodbyes.

Kate gave her a hug next. "We've lived in the same town for all our lives, and while I never thought we had anything in common, I was wrong," she said to Danielle. "I'm glad we were forced to work together so we could get to know each other. Throughout everything, you've held our group together through your strength and determination. You're one of the smartest people I know, and if there's a way back to Earth from Kerberos once the portal is sealed, you and Erebus will find it."

"Coming from a descendant of Athena, that means a lot," Danielle said.

"It's true," Kate said. "And Nicole's right. None of us will forget your sacrifice today. And when you and Erebus make it back—no matter if it takes one year or one thousand years—I'll be here waiting for you."

"Thank you," she said, and then she turned to Blake, her eyes brimming with sadness. "I guess this is it, isn't it?" she asked with a shrug.

"If you've changed your mind and want me to do this, it's okay," he told her. "I still will."

"No." She shook her head. "Thank you for the offer, but I think we all know that I'm the one who has to do this. I'm *glad* to do it, so I can keep all of you—and the rest of the world—safe. As strange as it sounds, doing this feels right. I think it's always been my destiny."

He nodded and moved to join me, reaching for my hand and giving it a small squeeze.

That one motion meant everything to me. Because he was here with me, and we would be by each other's sides for the rest of our lives. The portal to Kerberos might be closing, but together, we would make sure that all of the creatures that escaped were sent back to Tartarus, where they belonged.

"Okay." Danielle took a deep breath and turned to face the portal. "I'm ready to get this over with."

CHAPTER FIFTY-FIVE

Instead of elongating the process further, Danielle glanced back at us one last time, and then she stepped through the portal.

Since the portal was transparent, we saw her appear on the other side. She took a second to get her bearings, and then she turned around, facing us. Her hair blew behind her, and she stared out at us, her eyes gleaming with determination.

Despite her courage, I couldn't imagine how terrified she must feel.

Her mouth opened—she was trying to say something to us—but it was impossible to hear her through the portal. I pointed to my ear and shook my head, and she nodded in understanding.

Instead of trying to speak, she stepped forward and

hovered her hand along her side of the portal. Once it was there, she pointed to Blake, and he stepped forward and did the same.

She counted to three on her other hand, and then the portal glimmered with color—red on Blake's side, and blue on Danielle's. It glowed brighter and brighter, and then, just as quickly as it had lit up, the colors disappeared.

Danielle raised her hands and reached for the portal, but they pressed up against it, as if it were a glass wall. She must have been trying to see if Nyx was wrong—to see if she could come back to Earth after completing the binding. But it didn't work. She was trapped, her hands pressed flat against the surface, staring out at us in despair.

"Should I wait to seal the portal?" I asked the others. "It looks like she wants to come back. If I wait, the binding will fade, and she'll be able to return."

No one answered—I guessed they felt as confused as I did. Because even though I wanted to wait and let Danielle back through, I knew in my heart that there was no other way to close the portal. I'd known that since the Oracle had told us in the Underworld, although I hadn't wanted to admit it to myself then.

This was our only option. If Danielle came back, we would have to go through all of this again sometime before the summer solstice—and it wouldn't be any easier the second time.

But before I sealed the portal, I needed one last thing to happen.

Finally, a shadow appeared behind Danielle, solidifying to take the form of a god I recognized well—Erebus. He was dressed like he'd been when he guided us through Kerberos—dark jeans and a black t-shirt. He placed a hand on Danielle's shoulder, and she spun around, throwing herself into his arms and burying her head into his chest.

He held her tightly, and then he pulled away to look into her eyes. He said something to her—we couldn't hear *what* he said since the portal blocked all sound— and then he lowered his lips to hers in a long, sensual kiss. Being together seemed to come naturally to them —as if they'd done this many times before. But eventually they broke apart, and Erebus reached for Danielle's hand, as if letting us know he was there for her.

Her eyes met mine, and she nodded. Even though she couldn't speak to me, I knew what she was saying.

It was time for me to seal the portal to Kerberos.

I stepped forward and placed my hand on the portal. It was warm—as if it still burned with Blake's fiery, red energy.

It was crazy to think that once I did this, we would be free of the threat of Kerberos forever. That everything we'd fought for these past few months would be over.

But I was thinking too much. I knew what needed to be done—I just needed to *do* it.

So I closed my eyes and focused on white energy. It was everywhere around me, and as always, it came to me easily, filling my body with its warmth and comfort. At the same time as I gathered the energy, I sent it out of my palm and into the portal. The portal grew hotter and hotter under my skin, but it didn't burn me. Instead, it called for me, asking for more. It was soaking in the white energy as if it were the most natural thing in the world, and I called forth more of it into my body, allowing it to flow through me and into the portal. Heat radiated against my face, and even though my eyes were closed, I knew the portal was glowing with my bright, white energy.

Suddenly the portal zapped me, and I yanked my hand back, yelping and opening my eyes.

I stepped back in shock. Because the portal was gone. Only the cave wall remained.

"What happened?" I asked, resting my hand back on the same spot I'd been touching before. It was rocky and cold—as if nothing else had ever existed here at all.

"You did it." Blake stepped up behind me, placed his hand over mine, and drew my palm off the wall. "You sealed the portal to Kerberos."

EPILOGUE: KATE

THREE MONTHS LATER

I stared up at the arched entrance to the Emerson-Abbot Academy, amazed by how far we'd come these past few months. With the blacksmith god Hephaestus's help, we'd built the New Alexandrian Library into a boarding school for demigods and witches. Now, here it stood—the dorms, classrooms, auditorium, and training grounds—hidden in the Virginian mountains and ready for students to arrive next week.

The buildings were inspired by the architecture of ancient Greece, making them look like they'd been plucked from the past. Qualified witches had been brought in as teachers, Darius had been appointed Headmaster, and I'd finally realized where I belonged in the pantheon of the gods—as the goddess of witches and demigods. I would be the patron goddess of the school, dedicating my immortal life to the education of young witches and demigods. After all, with so many escaped monsters roaming the world, it was more important than ever for the demigods who had recently come into their powers to be located, and for them and the witches to be trained for the dangers to come.

I walked through the archway and spotted Helios trimming the bushes along the sidewalk. He was doing a surprisingly good job, but I waved a hand in the air, using my power to cause the bush behind him to grow into an absolute mess.

"Great job, Helios!" I called out to him. "But don't forget the bush behind you. I think you missed it the first time around."

He turned around, spotted the overgrown bush, and mumbled incoherently. I just smiled and continued on my way.

True to the promise of the gods, Helios had been returned to us as a powerless human after we'd sealed the portal to Kerberos. He now worked under our command as the janitor of the school.

I opened the doors to the main building, amazed that in only a week, students would be entering these halls for the first time. In the center of the lobby were podiums holding the two statues that Blake, Nicole, and I had decided to erect—one of Danielle Emerson, and the other of Chris Abbot. Danielle stood fierce and proud, a replica of the Golden Sword gleaming in her hand. (She'd taken the real sword with her to Kerberos.) Chris's hands were raised, his hair and clothes blowing around him, as if he were using his power over the air. He was smiling, looking as happy and carefree as ever.

I brushed my fingers across the nameplate on his podium, my eyes filling with tears. Not a day had passed when I didn't miss him so much that it hurt. At least I knew that his soul was safe in Elysium. But as an immortal, I would never see him again, since I would never go to the Underworld myself.

All I could hope was that as time passed, the pain of his loss would fade, until I could look back on our time together and feel only happiness and appreciation that we had time together at all.

But for now, staring at his statue for too long hurt, so I glanced up at the beautiful mural that had just been completed on the ceiling. In it, Hypatia rode the back of a dragon, surrounded by all the dragons that had helped us in our fight against Typhon. She, like Danielle and Chris, would never be forgotten here.

The dragons' loyalty wouldn't be forgotten, either. After starting to build the school, we'd been thrilled to discover that their deaths didn't mean the extinction of their race. There was a community of dragons that hadn't been banished to Kerberos after the Second

Rebellion, who had been living on Earth alongside humans for centuries. Dragons had the ability to sense the magic in others, so they could find and locate demigods and witches. Per our command, Helios had called upon the last living dragons in the world and requested that they work with us to seek out missing demigods. We told them of our mission, and they were happy to help.

Because our mission was important. All over the world were demigods like Nicole, Ethan, and Rachael who had only recently come into their powers. They didn't understand who they were or what they could do. If they were coerced to the side of darkness, like Ethan had been, they could cause great destruction. It was vital that we found them and made sure that didn't happen. Also, monsters could sense their magic, and if those monsters found them first, they attacked to kill. So it was now our job to travel the world, find the demigods and witches, and bring them here so they could be safe while learning about their heritages and abilities alongside others like themselves.

Well, it wasn't *my* job. It was Nicole and Blake's. They'd been having the summer of their lives, riding the backs of dragons on the search for hidden demigods. Or demigods on the run because they were afraid of what they could do with their powers, like the first two they'd found—Sydney, a daughter of

Aphrodite, and Garrett, a son of Hermes. They, along with a few others, were already situated in their dorms and had started their training.

Nicole and Blake weren't going to be happy when school began and they would be forced into classrooms again—after all, they still needed to keep up with their regular education—but it was part of my job to ensure that all of the demigods and witches at this school received a proper human education along with their magical training. Just because Nicole and Blake had powers over the elements and had helped stop the war against the Titans, it didn't mean they could be excused from school forever.

Some of the adult demigods could take over their job during the week. And I would allow them to fly off in search of lost demigods on the weekends, because truth be told, those two thrived on adventure. It was where they excelled—it was where they felt alive. It wouldn't be fair to keep them grounded *all* the time.

I, on the other hand, was glad to have found a home at the place where I was the happiest—here, at school.

And not just at *any* school, but the school that I founded—The Emerson-Abbot Academy for Demigods and Witches.

FROM THE AUTHOR

I hope you enjoyed *Elementals 5: The Hands of Time*—the conclusion to the *Elementals* series! If so, I'd love if you left a review. Reviews help readers find the book, and I read each and every one of them.

If you're not ready to leave the *Elementals* world yet, I've written a short story about an adventure that another group of witches had on the night of the Olympian Comet.

To grab the ebook of the short story for FREE, visit michellemadow.com/elementals-short-story.

While the *Elementals* series is complete, I'm currently working on another series that takes place in the

Elementals world: *Elementals Academy.* Look out for *Elementals Academy* in 2022.

If you want an email from me when new books of mine release, go to www.michellemadow.com/subscribe and sign up for my email list.

In the meantime, I have lots of other series' for you to enjoy! All of them can be found on Amazon.

Young Adult Urban Fantasy
The Vampire Wish
The Angel Trials
The Faerie Games
The Dragon Twins

Young Adult Paranormal Romance
The Transcend Time Saga

Young Adult Contemporary Romance
The Secret Diamond Sisters

Young Adult Fantasy Standalones
Collide
Demon Kissed

ABOUT THE AUTHOR

Michelle Madow is a *USA Today* bestselling author of fast-paced fantasy novels that will leave you turning the pages wanting more! Her books are full of magic, adventure, romance, and twists you'll never see coming.

Michelle grew up in Maryland, and now lives in Florida. She's loved reading for as long as she can remember. She wrote her first book in her junior year of college and hasn't stopped writing since! She also loves traveling, and has been to all seven continents. Someday, she hopes to travel the world for a year on a cruise ship.

Connect with Michelle:

Facebook Group: facebook.com/
groups/michellemadow
Instagram: @michellemadow
Email: michelle@madow.com
Website: www.michellemadow.com

ELEMENTALS 5: The Hands of Time

Published by Dreamscape Publishing

Copyright © 2016 Michelle Madow

ISBN: 978-0-578-98860-3